Date
A Live
Change Natsumi

"I'm Chiyogami Itsuka. Thank you for always being so nice to my dad."

"Oh, you! Aaaah,
I said. Aaaah!"

Miku
A Spirit

"Th-this is...me?"

Natsumi
A Spirit

"Yup. No mistake. It's you, Natsumi."

Shiori Itsuka
A high school student

"Now, shall we begin our battle?"

Kotori Itsuka
Ratatoskr Commander

"**…A mom, huh?**"

Reine Murasame
Ratatoskr Analyst

CONTENTS

Date A Live
Change Natsumi

09

Koushi Tachibana

Illustrated by
Tsunako

YEN
ON

New York

Koushi Tachibana

Translation by Jocelyne Allen
Cover art by Tsunako

This book is a work of fiction. Names, characters, places, and incidents are the product of the author's imagination or are used fictitiously. Any resemblance to actual events, locales, or persons, living or dead, is coincidental.

DATE A LIVE Vol.9 CHANGE NATSUMI
©Koushi Tachibana, Tsunako 2013
First published in Japan in 2013 by KADOKAWA CORPORATION, Tokyo.
English translation rights arranged with KADOKAWA CORPORATION, Tokyo through TUTTLE-MORI AGENCY, Inc., Tokyo.

English translation © 2023 by Yen Press, LLC

Yen On
150 West 30th Street, 19th Floor
New York, NY 10001

Visit us at yenpress.com
facebook.com/yenpress
twitter.com/yenpress
yenpress.tumblr.com
instagram.com/yenpress

First Yen On Edition: June 2023
Edited by Yen On Editorial: Ivan Liang
Designed by Yen Press Design: Andy Swist

Yen On is an imprint of Yen Press, LLC.
The Yen On name and logo are trademarks of Yen Press, LLC.

The publisher is not responsible for websites (or their content) that are not owned by the publisher.

Library of Congress Cataloging-in-Publication Data
Names: Tachibana, Koushi, 1986– author. | Tsunako, illustrator. | Allen, Jocelyne, 1974– translator.
Title: Date a live / Koushi Tachibana ; illustration by Tsunako ; translation by Jocelyne Allen.
Other titles: Dēto a raibu. English
Description: First Yen On edition. | New York, NY : Yen On, 2021–
Identifiers: LCCN 2020054696 | ISBN 9781975319915 (v. 1 ; trade paperback) |
    ISBN 9781975319939 (v. 2 ; trade paperback) | ISBN 9781975319953 (v. 3 ; trade paperback) |
    ISBN 9781975319977 (v. 4 ; trade paperback) | ISBN 9781975319991 (v. 5 ; trade paperback) |
    ISBN 9781975320010 (v. 6 ; trade paperback) | ISBN 9781975348298 (v. 7 ; trade paperback) |
    ISBN 9781975349943 (v. 8 ; trade paperback) | ISBN 9781975350307 (v. 9 ; trade paperback)
Subjects: GSAFD: Science fiction. | Fantasy fiction.
Classification: LCC PL876.A23 D4813 2021 | DDC 895.63/6—dc23
LC record available at https://lccn.loc.gov/2020054696

ISBNs: 978-1-9753-5030-7 (paperback)
       978-1-9753-5031-4 (ebook)

10 9 8 7 6 5 4 3 2 1

LSC-C

Printed in the United States of America

Spirit

A uniquely catastrophic creature existing in a parallel world. Cause of occurrence and reason for existence unknown. Creates a spacequake and inflicts serious damage on her surroundings whenever she appears in this world. A very powerful fighter.

Strategy No. 1

Annihilate with force. This approach is very difficult, since the Spirit is extremely powerful, as noted above.

Strategy No. 2

...Date her and make her all weak in the knees.

Change Natsumi

Spirit No. 7
Astral Dress—Witch Type
Weapon—Broom Type [Haniel]

Chapter 6
Little Monsters

Sunday, October 29. Chaos reigned at the Itsuka house.

"Shido! I'm hungwyyyyyy!"

"Shido, potty. I can't by myself. Come, Shido."

"Daaarling! Daaaaarling!"

"Uh. Umm… Shido…"

"Everyone, calm down! Ah, Kaguya! That'th my Chupa Chupth!"

"Shido! I wanna eat! Wight now!"

"Keh-keh, wee one. Clinging to mere triwialities does nothing but expose your own stunted nature."

"Assent. We can have one at least."

"You too?! Give that back!"

"Ungh! Waaaaaaah!"

"Aah! Now look what you did! There, there."

"Shido, I'm gonna pee my pants."

"Keeeh-keh-keh-keh! That which has once entered our domain can never be weturned!"

"Escape. If you wish us to weturn them, then you'd do well to catch us."

"…" Shido cradled his head in his hands silently, a trickle of sweat running down his cheek.

He already had a headache from lack of sleep, and the constant piercing screams and the stamping of little feet were definitely not helping. Not to mention that after tiny hands had yanked the hem of his shirt so hard and in so many directions, Shido was left wearing a stretched-out mess.

In the Itsuka living room at the moment, there were technically seven little girls, but it would've been more accurate to call them demons. All seemed under ten, an age that was a handful even at the best of times. They wept and shouted and tugged on Shido and chased one another around the house. It was only too easy to guess at how exhausted Shido was after he'd been pressed into watching the girls a few days earlier.

Of course, he had no choice in the matter. The girls weren't girls because they wanted to be. Shido let out a short sigh before lifting his head and turning his eyes on the little monsters running wild in the living room.

The girl who kept shouting about how hungry she felt was beautiful, boasting long hair the color of the night and crystalline eyes. The girl with a face as expressionless as a doll's was pestering Shido to take her to the bathroom. The girl with a familiar puppet on her left hand looked ready to burst into tears at any second. The girl with her hair in pigtails had a Chupa Chups in her mouth and a determined expression. The girl running away after stealing the candy clearly had a mischievous streak. The girl with a blank look on her face was a perfect copy of the mischievous girl. The girl with a beautiful voice was a little taller than the others.

They would have been adorable if they weren't causing so much mayhem. But that wasn't the real issue. Shido looked at each of them once more and swallowed hard.

He knew these faces. They had the exact same features as his friends and family: Tohka, Origami, Yoshino, Miku, Kaguya, Yuzuru, and Kotori.

Anyone who didn't know about recent events would rightfully assume these little gremlins were younger relatives or simply bore an uncanny resemblance to the girls. But Shido knew the truth: These kids were the real deal.

This sort of thing would normally have been unthinkable. In general, living creatures grew physically with the passage of time; in other words, they aged. And yet Tohka and the rest had all turned into children, as though their lives had been rewound several years. Actually, that description might not have been entirely accurate. Shido didn't know if Tohka, Yoshino, and the other Spirits matured the same way human beings did. He couldn't say for sure whether or not they had ever experienced a childhood stage like this. For them, rather than rewinding time, they had simply been given children's bodies. And the one responsible for all this was a Spirit with a nefarious ability.

"Natsumi, why on earth would you...?" Shido murmured to himself as he thought of a certain witch.

A few days earlier, a Spirit named Natsumi had challenged him to a contest, and he'd won. But the moment he did, Natsumi transformed everyone in the room into children and then flew off somewhere. As a result, the Itsuka household had become a strange sort of day care ever since.

"Shido! Shido!"

"Shido, I can't hold it much longer."

"Ungh. Waaah!"

"Hey! Thtop right there!"

"Mwa-ha-ha! You are free to come and stop me!"

"Sneer. Is that all you got?"

"Daaarliiiing! Daaarliiiing!"

"Okay! Yes! I get it! Everyone, just simmer down for one second!" Shido shouted, rocking back and forth as different hands pulled him in every direction. But the girls kept clamoring.

"...Excuse me."

Just as Shido was nearing the end of his rope like the teacher of a class gone wild, the living room door opened abruptly, and a woman stepped through.

Her hair had been pulled back rather haphazardly, and there were impressive bags under her sleepy eyes. A stuffed bear that had clearly been darned and restitched many times sat in her breast pocket. This was Shido's assistant homeroom teacher and analyst of the secret organization Ratatoskr, Reine Murasame.

"Reine!" he cried with relief.

"...Looks like you've got your hands full, Shin," Reine said. She scanned the living room to get an idea of what was going on, and then she slowly held out her hands to catch the collars of the Yamai sisters racing around the living room, stopping them in their tracks.

"Nwaaah?!"

"Impact. Hgah!"

Coming to a hard stop, Kaguya and Yuzuru wore bewildered looks on their faces.

Reine calmly knelt down, looked them in the eyes, and began to gently lecture them. "...Kaguya, Yuzuru. You can't take other people's things. You wouldn't like it if someone else went and ate your candy, would you?"

The twins stammered uncomfortably.

"Mmmgh..."

"Remorse. I'm sorry."

"...Good. Now both of you, tell Kotori you're sorry." Reine patted Kaguya and Yuzuru on the shoulders.

The twins turned toward Kotori and bowed their heads.

"Hmph. Sorry, I guess."

"Apology. We won't do it again."

"...How's that, Kotori? We'll make sure to replace the candy they took later. Could you maybe forgive them?" Reine turned her gaze toward Kotori, who sniffed indignantly as she crossed her arms.

"D-doesn't matter now. Whatever... I'm sorry, too, for not sharing."

"...Mm. You're all good kids." Reine stroked each girl's hair in turn, and Kotori, Kaguya, and Yuzuru averted their eyes awkwardly.

"...Now then, I wonder what's going on over here."

Next, Reine walked over to Shido and turned her gaze on Tohka, Origami, Yoshino, and Miku, all of whom were clinging to him. After hearing them all out, she started talking in a calm, measured voice.

"...Tohka, Shin's just a bit busy right now. Can you wait a little longer for supper? I'll give you this cookie as a special treat if you can do that. Origami, Shin said he likes girls who can go potty by themselves. Yoshino, don't worry. Shin isn't upset that you broke that dish this morning. Miku, Shin is definitely listening to you. He would never ignore you."

She spoke to each one of them in turn and easily soothed their tiny tantrums. This was the deft work of a master.

"Thanks," Shido said. "You're a lifesaver. They're too much for me alone."

"...Not at all," Reine replied. "I feel bad for leaving you to take care of all of them."

"Nah, I know you're looking for Natsumi. Still..." Shido looked over the now-quiet girls and smiled wryly. "You're really amazing, Reine. You're like a mom with them."

"..." Reine only moved her eyebrows slightly, without saying a word.

Shido gasped. He hadn't meant anything by the offhand comment. In fact, he'd said every word with nothing but respect, but when he considered it, this was not exactly the sort of thing someone should say thoughtlessly to an unmarried woman. He hurriedly waved his hands and corrected himself. "I-I'm sorry. That's not what I meant. I wasn't trying to say..."

"...No, it's fine." Reine didn't seem particularly bothered. But her face was generally hard to read, so he couldn't really tell if she was actually upset or not.

"S-so anyway. Did you find Natsumi?" he said to change the subject.

Reine lowered her eyes and shook her head. "...It seems that Natsumi is able to mask her Spirit signal. I've got the measurement devices spreading a wide net, but we still haven't picked anything up. Of course, it's also possible she's been Lost to the parallel world already."

"I...guess that's possible," Shido agreed, as he looked at the gaggle of girls in his care. Until they found Natsumi, the cause of all this chaos, they were going to be stuck like this. He turned his gaze back on Reine. "But why would Natsumi do this?"

"...That's the big question." Reine nodded. "It might have been an emergency measure to allow her to escape the scene. It could also be that she was giving you a warning of some kind by reducing the Spirits' fighting abilities. Or..."

"Or?" Shido cocked his head to one side, and Reine held up a finger.

"...maybe she just wanted to cause as much trouble as possible."

"..." Shido stiffened at this. Although Reine had said it as a joke, he couldn't help but feel that this was the true answer to his question.

The UK was about twelve hours away by plane from Heathrow Airport to Japan's Narita Airport.

Having taken care of the last of his duties in the cabin of his private jet, Isaac Westcott exited the exclusive terminal, climbed into a waiting car, and headed toward the hotel in Tengu where he would be staying while he was in the greater Tokyo area.

He was a tall man with dark ash-blond hair and eyes as sharp as a naked blade. He looked to be somewhere in his midthirties, but the daunting presence he projected almost made him seem older. If nothing else, no one who had met him in person had ever walked away thinking he was too young to stand at the top of a global corporation like DEM Industries.

"These back-to-back trips are quite exhausting, hmm?" Westcott said, rolling his shoulders slightly. "What do you think, Ellen? Should we make Japan our permanent residence?"

The Nordic blond girl sitting beside him narrowed her eyes. "I would have actually preferred to postpone this trip. I'm quite frankly impressed that you would leave your own castle empty after an incident like *that*."

Her tone was harsh. This was Ellen M. Mathers, head of the second enforcement division and DEM Industries' shadow executive who answered directly to Westcott.

"Such praise!" Westcott said. "I'm blushing."

"That wasn't praise," Ellen replied curtly, and the older man shrugged.

Naturally, he understood perfectly well what she was driving at. A few days earlier at the DEM Industries UK head office, there had been a call for Westcott's dismissal during the board meeting. He'd managed to skate past that proposal thanks to Ellen's *physical* persuasiveness, but the fact that he was frequently away from the head office was an issue. His absences gave the upstart board members plenty of time to prepare their little plots, and there was no love lost between them and Westcott. It was plenty possible that they would turn on him once again in some fashion or another. In light of that, Ellen's testiness was only natural.

Westcott's expression softened. "Personally, I don't mind a whit. I prefer working with people ambitious enough to come for me and try to rip out my throat given the slightest opportunity to do so."

"Perhaps you take no issue with that, but please consider the position of the one who must clean up afterward." Ellen pursed her lips ever so slightly in dissatisfaction.

"I'll tread carefully," Westcott replied. "Did you look into that matter for me?"

"Yes. Here." Ellen sighed, pulled a bundle of papers clipped together out of her bag, and handed it to Westcott.

He took the stack and pored over the photographs and lines of text printed on the papers. These were the results of the investigation into this boy Shido Itsuka and his background.

"I see. So he was adopted by this family some years ago. And the little sister is suspected to be the Spirit Efreet. How nice of them to come together like this. Or perhaps better to say they were *put* together, hmm?" Westcott chuckled and flipped through the documents. The next page had photos of several girls. "Princess, Hermit, Berserk, Diva, and the aforementioned Efreet. He's collected six confirmed Spirits. Ellen, what does this look like to you?"

"Like Ratatoskr is most definitely involved," Ellen replied, letting the tiniest bit of her displeasure show.

"No doubt about that, hmm?" Westcott agreed. "A boy who can seal the power of a Spirit—Ratatoskr would certainly have a use for that. And to lock up this many Spirits on his own, well, he might have an unusual ability, but without the backing of a vast organization, he wouldn't even be able to make contact with the Spirits. However..." Westcott cut himself off and tapped the page with a finger. "Is that really the whole story?"

"Meaning?" Ellen asked, arching an eyebrow slightly.

Westcott shrugged. "Just what I said. Is this odd, twisted situation solely the work of our rival Ratatoskr?"

"Are you implying there's someone else pulling the strings behind the scenes?"

"Who can say? If, however, there *was* such a mastermind, it wouldn't change the work we have to do. Isn't that right, Ellen? Ellen M. Mathers, humanity's most powerful Wizard."

Ellen stared at Westcott for a few seconds as if trying to discern his true intention before dropping her head in a nod. "Of course." There wasn't a hint of uncertainty or hesitation on her face.

Westcott nodded with satisfaction. "Then we'd best get to it. You'll move as soon as everything's in place."

"Yes, sir," Ellen said, lowering her eyes to the document in Westcott's hand. "Who exactly shall we begin with? Will it be Princess?"

"No." Westcott shook his head. "I'd like to leave the Spirits in this document some rope for the time being. Although naturally, I don't mind if you take their heads should the opportunity present itself."

"What do you mean by that?" Ellen asked.

Westcott pointed at the picture of Princess, aka Tohka Yatogami. "The memory of Princess inverting is still fresh, our beloved king's first appearance."

"Yes."

"That inversion was caused by none other than this boy, Shido Itsuka. When you tried to kill him, Princess stood on the precipice and demanded power greater than anything she herself possessed. As a result, she was able to grab onto Nahemah, the sword of the demon king."

Westcott set the papers down in his lap and spread out his arms.

"Who could have imagined the king we have yearned for all this time would come to us so easily? The Spirits value, trust, and love this boy from the bottom of their hearts—or at least, Princess does. Isn't that marvelous? So let's have them push this relationship even further to build even greater trust. For when the time comes, hmm?"

At this point, Ellen grasped Westcott's intentions. With no change in the expression on her face, she dipped her head forward in agreement.

The deeper the relationship between Shido Itsuka and the Spirits, the more the Spirits depended on Shido Itsuka, the more powerful their despair would be at the threat of losing him. Powerful enough for them to reach for strength that could not be contained in their own domain.

"Do you intend to use Shido Itsuka as a key?" Ellen asked.

"Key? Yes, that a good way of putting it." Westcott smiled slightly. "Ironic, isn't it? That the secret anti-Spirit weapon Ratatoskr dug up could become our joker."

"Medicine easily turns to poison depending on the dose. However..."

Westcott knew what this meant without her having to spell it out for him. Basically, if this was the case, then which Spirit should Ellen pick to start the hunt?

He nodded exaggeratedly. "Yes, a priority target has already been set. In an impeccable bit of timing, we received a report from the AST the other day. Witch, a Spirit with the power of transformation, manifested in the suburbs of Tengu and has yet to be confirmed as Lost."

"Morning."

The next morning, Shido stepped into the Itsuka living room, yawning hugely.

Given that he couldn't exactly send the child versions of the girls back to their apartments in the building next door, they'd split up between Shido's room (Shido, Tohka, Yoshino, Miku) and Kotori's room (Kotori, Kaguya, Yuzuru), with everyone sleeping together on the floor. But Yoshino and Miku clung to him all night long, and then Tohka climbed on to his chest, so he hadn't really slept at all.

But not all the girls stayed over at the Itsuka house. Origami said she had some things to take care of and had reluctantly returned home, dragging her feet.

Now that he was thinking about it, Shido realized he'd been missing a bunch of things since then, like his underpants and toothbrush. But when exactly had he lost them?

"Morning, Shido."

"Good moooorning, daaaaarling."

"G-good…morning…"

"Yup. *It's a great morning, huh?*"

Kotori, Miku, Yoshino, and Yoshinon were already in the living room.

"Whoa, you're all up early, huh?" Shido said, as the three girls and one puppet looked at him curiously.

"It's important to take care of yourself."

"Um. I always…get up at this time."

"Early bed, early rise is your skin's best friend. It's only naaaatural for me as an idol."

Kotori crossed her arms and rolled her eyes, Yoshino shrank into herself as if embarrassed, and Miku spoke smugly as she caressed her own cheeks. They might have been turned into children, but that apparently had not disrupted their daily rhythms.

Shido remembered the happy look on Tohka's sleeping face as he left his bedroom and automatically smiled. The fact that she wasn't here now no doubt meant that she and the Yamai sisters had gone back to sleep in Kotori's room. It was weirdly adorable.

"Okay, give me a minute. I'll have breakfast ready in a jiff," he said, as he put on an apron before washing his hands and getting started on their morning meal.

He mixed eggs, milk, and sugar together in a bowl, cut some bread into bite-size pieces, soaked them in the egg mix, then fried them until they were crispy in a pan with a pat of butter. Simple and delicious, easy French toast. Naturally, he didn't forget to whip up a salad and some soup while the bread was soaking. Within twenty minutes, a heavenly aroma was wafting through the Itsuka house.

"It'll be ready in a little bit, so clear off the table," he called out.

""""Okay!""""

The three girls jumped into action. Yoshino put away all the random objects on the table, Kotori covered it with a tablecloth, and Miku brought out plates with food piled on them. It wasn't a particularly unusual morning scene, but maybe because they were all little now, it felt curiously like watching some cute kids helping out.

"How about we dig in, then?" Shido said. .

""""Yeah!""""

The three girls copied Shido and clapped their hands in thanks for the food before lifting their forks to their faces.

"It's…yummy…!" Yoshino's eyes flew open when she popped a piece of French toast in her mouth.

"Mm. Not bad." Kotori sniffed, not unsatisfied. Whatever they said, Shido was just happy they were enjoying his cooking. His face softened into a smile as he stabbed at his own plate with a fork.

"Hey, daaaarling? Daaaaaaarling?" Miku tugged on his sleeve from where she sat next to him.

"Hmm? What's up, Miku?" he asked.

Miku clasped her hands in front of her chest, lowered her eyes, and opened her mouth. "Aaaah."

"Huh?"

"Oh, you! Aaaah, I said. Aaaah!" She huffed in anger before opening her mouth once more.

"O-ohhh…" He cut a piece of toast and brought it to her mouth.

"Mmmm!" She pressed her hands to her cheeks and cried out in delight. "It's wonderful! It's totally different when you feeeeed me, darling!"

"Ha-ha... I doubt the taste changes, though." Shido smiled awkwardly and turned back to his plate when he realized that Kotori and Yoshino were wearing indignant looks on their faces.

"All three of you?" he asked, and Kotori and Yoshino furrowed their brows, troubled.

"Mmm."

Then...

"*Hup!*"

"Eeah?!"

Who knew what the puppet was thinking? Yoshinon abruptly delivered a sharp chop to Yoshino's right hand, knocking her fork right out of it.

"H-hey, Yoshinon?" Shido asked.

"*Aaaah! Sorry, Shidoooo. Yoshino's fork fell because Yoshinon was so careless. Could you maybe feed her, too? Sorry about that.*"

"Um...?" He raised a skeptical eyebrow. "I don't mind, but I could just get you a new fork..."

"*Could. You. Maybe. Feed. Yoshino. Too?*" Yoshinon said, looming in close and letting the implicit threat hang in the air.

Shido nodded. "S-sure..."

"Oh. Um... Shido... I'm...sorry."

"Nah, it's not your fault, Yoshino." He held out a fork with a piece of toast on it. "Here. Say 'aaah.'"

"A-aaah..." She hesitantly opened her mouth wide and bit down on the toast. After chewing and swallowing, she smiled, a little embarrassed. "Thank...you. It's...really...good."

"Yeah? Glad to hear it." He smiled, replaced Yoshino's fork, and turned to his own plate once more. However.

"Hmph..."

Kotori was staring across the table at him with eyes so watery, she looked ready to start weeping at the drop of a hat. Shido would have to put off eating once again.

"Uhhh."

He knew the score. It was probably because she had been turned into a child, but he felt like Kotori's mood swings were even easier to pick up on than usual. Just like he had with Miku and Yoshino, Shido cut off a piece of toast and held it out to her. "Come on, Kotori. Say 'aah.'"

"...! I—I never asked for this," she snapped. "Could you not treat me like a child?!"

"But...you *are* a child."

"Hmph!" Kotori pouted for half a second and then snatched the toast from the fork with her mouth. She swallowed it, pursed her lips, and lowered her eyes. "Thanks."

"Sure thing. You're welcome," Shido said, and was finally about to pop some of this French toast into his own mouth when the living room door flew open. Tohka stepped inside, looking extremely sleepy.

"Mmngh. There's a...yummy smell," she said, and then yawned.

This was simply too on-brand for Tohka. Shido and the others looked at one another and burst out laughing.

"Though anyway, what are you planning to do today?" Kotori asked Shido, in a much better mood now that they'd all had breakfast.

Meanwhile, Tohka had flopped over on the sofa, sated by French toast, and was once again traveling through the land of dreams.

"Right," Shido started, scratching his cheek. "I figured I'd go to school for the time being. But there's also the whole thing with Natsumi, and I'm worried about leaving Tohka and everyone else alone. So I was planning to come home at lunch. I'm wondering about Tonomachi and the others, too."

It wasn't actually only this little group who'd gotten caught up in Natsumi's little games. Shido's classmates Hiroto Tonomachi, Ai Yamabuki, Mai Hazakura, and Mii Fujibakama, and their home-room teacher, Tamae Okamine, had also been locked inside the Angel temporarily by the Spirit. Fortunately, they hadn't been turned into children like Tohka and the others, but that didn't change the fact that Shido had involved them in a dangerous situation, whether he'd intended to or not. He wanted to see for himself that they were okay after they regained consciousness.

"Oh, okay," Kotori said. "Still, we don't know where Natsumi is. You be careful."

"Yeah, I will." He nodded. "I should get going. When Kaguya and Yuzuru wake up, heat some breakfast for them. The French toast is better when it's hot from the pan, but I'm scared to let you use the stove."

"I *told* you, I'm not a child—" Kotori cut herself off, then grimaced in dissatisfaction as she nodded.

Shido patted her head as if to say "good girl" (and naturally, Miku and Yoshino pestered him to do the same for them) before he put on his blazer and got ready to leave. He slid his feet into his shoes as he put a hand on the doorknob.

"Okay, you're in charge," he said, looking back at Kotori. "I'll have my earpiece in, so call if anything happens."

"Yeah, yeah, got it." She flapped a dismissive hand at him.

Yoshino waved shyly. "Have a…good day."

"Daaarling, where's my kiss? Where's my good-bye kiiiiss?" Miku thrust her lips out at him.

Smiling awkwardly, Shido waved at all three, opened the door, and stepped outside.

The weather was good. In stark contrast to the complicated situation Shido and his friends found themselves in, the day was pleasantly sunny.

"Mm." Shido stretched as if to expose his entire body to the sun and then started walking to school.

"…?"

But he had barely stepped beyond the front gate when he abruptly stopped again. And shifted his gaze to the right, then the left. He cocked his head to one side.

"There's no one here…right?"

For a moment, Shido felt like someone's eyes were on him. But maybe it was all in his head. He *was* on edge due to the whole Natsumi thing. Shido took a deep breath to calm his racing heart before setting out for school once more.

"Listen, Itsuka! The most incredible, unbelievable thing happened to me!" A boy with his hair waxed straight up raced over to him excitedly the second Shido stepped into Class 4. Hiroto Tonomachi, one of the students disappeared by Natsumi's mirror. From the look of him, it didn't seem like there was anything wrong with him physically at least. Heaving a sigh of relief inside, Shido rolled his eyes at his friend.

"What's up with you, Tonomachi?" he asked. "You remember you're the son of Bigfoot or something?"

"You *get* it! Seriously, the hair on my arm's been growing kind of— No, wait, hold up." Tonomachi shook his head vigorously. "That's not it! An alien, man! *Aliens!*"

"Aliens?" Shido raised a dubious eyebrow. "Oh, is that it? I just assumed you were a cryptid, but to think you're actually an alien—"

"No, no!" Tonomachi protested. "*I'm* not the alien! I went to sleep on the night of the twenty-fifth, but when I woke up again, it was the twenty-eighth!"

"Whoa, man. Maybe you're sleeping just a *teensy* bit too much?"

"Yes! It's weird, right?! It's actually a huge mystery!" Tonomachi cried. "I wake up to find whole days have gone by, and on top of that, I asked my family, and they said I totally disappeared, man! They literally reported me missing! I freaked!"

"And so, aliens," Shido said flatly.

"Yeah! I mean, can you think of anything else?!"

Shido scratched his head. There was no doubt in his mind that Tonomachi was talking about the period of time when he was held captive by Natsumi's Angel. But he couldn't actually tell his friend this. Even if he did come out and say to his friend, "No, Tonomachi, that wasn't the work of aliens; it was actually a Spirit. You were held captive inside a Spirit's Angel. Incidentally, the spacequakes are also because of the Spirits. And the truth is, I happen to be able to seal away their power," the end result would be Tonomachi giving him some very strange looks and walking far, far away. So he settled on staring at Tonomachi dubiously. Whatever else, he was glad his friend was okay.

Three girls abruptly pushed their way into Shido's field of vision. They had overheard Tonomachi's excited prattling.

"Oooh! Hey, hey!"

"*This*, I gotta hear about!"

"You're part of the mystery tour group, too, Tonomachi?"

They were Tohka's friends and, like Tonomachi, had also been dragged into the whole guessing game. In order of tallest to shortest, Ai, Mai, Mii.

"Huh? So you mean the same thing happened to you, too?" Tonomachi asked, and Ai-Mai-Mii bobbed their heads up and down.

"Yeah, totally, exactly. But no one will believe us, y'know?"

"We can't remember the last couple days at all!"

"So it really *is* aliens? Or maybe the work of some mysterious organization?"

The girls squealed one after the other.

"That reminds me! Tama was saying she had the same thing!"

"What? For real? That can't be a coincidence."

"So then that's five of us. I smell a conspiracy!"

"No way! Were we really kidnapped by some secret society?!"

"Did they mod us so we have superhuman powers now?!"

"And five of us… We got a superhero-team situation here!"

Ai-Mai-Mii all struck deliberate poses, like they'd been practicing for this.

"C'mon! You too, Red!"

"U-uh?!" Tonomachi yelped, as the girls yanked him over and forced him to pose with them.

"Okay, we join forces and defeat the evil humanoid running rampant!"

"Evil humanoid…?" Tonomachi asked.

"Yep!" Ai, Mai, or Mii said. "A humanoid pretending to be a person has already snuck into our midst and is doing his evil deeds!"

"More specifically, he's doing stuff like grabbing a girl's breasts, flipping up skirts, and trying to steal kisses!"

"En garde! Obscene humanoid Shido Itsuka!"

"Me?!" Shido jumped where he stood when they whirled around to focus their ire on him.

Maybe the girls were still holding a grudge over the antics that Natsumi had gotten up to while disguised as a perfect copy of Shido.

"I-is that it, Itsuka?" Tonomachi stammered. "I *thought* you'd been acting weird lately."

"So you know something!" Ai-Mai-Mii cried.

"Y-yeah." Tonomachi nodded slowly. "Not long before my memory cut out, I remember being kinda weirded out by how Itsuka was looking at me. And then he started inviting me to the sauna, coming over and touching me and stuff."

"Eek! Eek!"

"I-Itsuka, you like boys, too?!"

"Ogiiii! 'Fujoshi Best Couple Selection' Committee Chair Ogiiiii! We've got news that completely rewrites the rankings!"

"Itsuka." Tonomachi looked at Shido nervously. "So that *was* what was going on?"

"Oh, come on!" Shido cried. "Why are you joining in, Tonomachi? And, like, homeroom's starting."

As he spoke, the familiar bell rang throughout the school.

"See, look?" he said. "The teacher's here."

"Don't go trying to weasel out of this! Itsuka, you seriously—," Tonomachi said heatedly, ignoring the bell.

However.

"Oh! Homeroom!"

"Back to my desk with me!"

"What's first period today?"

Ai-Mai-Mii dropped the whole thing and walked away without

a second thought. They likely weren't aware of it, but they had left Tonomachi extremely high and dry.

Seeing this, Tonomachi sweated for a moment before also returning to his own desk. "O-okay, later."

Soon enough, the classroom door opened, and a small woman with glasses stepped inside. It was Shido's homeroom teacher, and the last of the five people from school trapped in Natsumi's mirror: educator Tamae Okamine, aka Tama.

Apparently, she was unharmed as well. Shido started to let out a sigh of relief, then frowned.

The reason was simple. Tama was clearly acting weird. Sweat beaded on her forehead, her eyes darted around the room, and she was obviously shaken. What exactly had happened?

As Shido studied her, Tama abruptly turned her gaze in his direction. And then after a moment of hesitation, she opened her mouth.

"Er... Itsuka?"

"Wh-what?" he replied.

Tama screwed up her face in confusion. "Oh, well, it's just that you have a visitor, and, um..."

"A visitor?" Shido tilted his head to one side. He couldn't think of anyone who would come and see him at school. He had the thought that it was someone from Ratatoskr, but in that case, they would've let him know through his earpiece.

"...!"

Two possibilities flashed through the back of his mind: DEM Industries and the Spirit Natsumi.

"Where is this visitor?" he demanded.

"Oh, right. In the teachers'—," Tama started to say.

"Shido!" an unbelievably excited voice called from the entrance to the classroom.

"Wha...?!" He turned his eyes in that direction and lost the power of speech momentarily.

Standing there was neither an assassin from DEM Industries nor

Natsumi, but rather a diminutive Tohka, the very one who was supposed to be asleep at his house.

Tama hurriedly stepped out in front of her. "Oh, no, you don't! I told you to wait in the teachers' office, now didn't I?"

"Mm?" Tohka raised an eyebrow. "Why, Tama? I'm not allowed in the classroom?"

"Well, you see, this is a place for big girls and boys to study, so..."

"I can study with Shido, too, you know!" Tohka declared.

"Er, maybe once you get a little bit bigger," Tama consoled Tohka awkwardly, and a small someone slipped out from behind Tohka.

"Keh-keh! What act is this?"

"Excuse. People are waiting."

"..."

Kaguya and Yuzuru, also meant to be fast asleep at his house, marched into the classroom together with Origami.

The classroom erupted in excitement at the appearance of these unexpected visitors. Reactions were broadly divided into three types: students who stared curiously and wondered, "Why are these little kids here?"; those who let out squeals of "Wah! They're so cute!"; and those who frowned with "Huh? I feel like I've seen these kids somewhere before."

In that moment, Shido heard Kotori's voice through his earpiece.

"—do! Shido! Can you hear me? It's an emergency! Tohka and the others disappeared from the house!"

He sighed. "Yeah. They came here."

"What?!"

Tohka turned toward Shido, and her face lit up like the sun as she leaped toward him.

"Ah, Shido! So you *are* hewe!"

Following her lead, Kaguya and Yuzuru also raced over to him.

"Oi, Shido!" Kaguya said. "You must speak to the homeroom teacher of Year Two, Class Three on our behalf. They doubt when we say we are Yamai."

"Sigh. They are an adult who can only comprehend appearances," Yuzuru said, shaking her head as she actually sighed instead of just saying it.

While all this was going on, Shido's classmates were whispering around him furiously. He couldn't hear everything they were saying, but he could pick out words like "Lolita complex," "crime," and "totally wrong."

It was blindingly obvious that the whispers were very bad, but he didn't have time to deal with them at the moment. He turned back to Tohka.

"What are you all doing here?" he asked.

"Mm? That's a weird question." She frowned at him. "Today's a school day. You slept with us, but then you disappeared. You scared me!"

"...?!"

Shido's classmates gasped in shock and horror and turned stunned gazes on Shido.

"Hey, Itsuka? Who *are* these kids?"

"What exactly is your relationship with them?"

"And, like, you're sleeping with them?"

Ai-Mai-Mii furrowed their brows, suspicious, as they looked back and forth between Shido and Tohka.

He hurriedly racked his brain for some kind of excuse. But before he could say anything, a small figure tottered over to him and embraced him tightly the way Tohka had. Origami.

"Papa."

A heartbeat after the shocking word was uttered, the entire class exploded into chaotic chatter.

"Wha...?!"

"Papa?! Did she just say 'Papa'?!"

"Huh? 'Papa'?! The Polynesian earth goddess?! The Greek scholar?!"

"Y-young lady, what's your name?" Ai asked gently, after she knelt down so that she could look Origami in the eye (although her eyes did dart about in confusion).

Origami bowed very politely. "I'm Chiyogami Itsuka. Thank you for always being so nice to my dad."

"Wh-whoa?!" Ai gasped.

"Mama's name is Origami Tobiichi," miniature Origami said, continuing. "I'm the result of Mama and Papa's love."

"*What?!*"

The stunned class began to whisper and chatter.

"N-now that you mention it, you *do* look like Tobiichi!"

"Huh? No way! Tobiichi gave birth when she's still in high school?!"

"No, but you can get married at sixteen, legally speaking..."

"For guys, it's eighteen, though! So Itsuka's done!"

"Wait. Hey. Doesn't this girl look like Yatogami? And the Yamais from the class next door!"

"What? You mean polygamy?!"

"B-but this doesn't make any sense? These kids are—what, eight or nine from the look of them? So they gave birth when they were eight years old?! Itsuka, did you knock up eight-year-old girls?!"

"Wait. But the record for the youngest birth ever is five years and seven months, so it's not impossible..."

"S-stop! This is all a misunderstanding!" Shido blasted at the top of his voice to end the conversation. The last thing he wanted was more weird rumors spreading about him. "These girls... Yes! Right! They're cousins! I'm just taking care of them! That whole 'papa' thing, i-i-it's like a nickname!"

"Whaaat?" All eyes were on him, and they were extremely dubious eyes.

To be honest, Shido himself was well aware that this was a ridiculous excuse, but if his classmates took a breath and really thought about it, they would realize at the very least that there was no way Shido, as a high schooler, could have children this age. The looks on their faces said that his story wasn't sitting too well with them, but they accepted it at any rate.

"Hmm. Cousins, huh? I mean, we're talking about Itsuka here, so I was just like, oh, I guess he could have kids."

"Right? It seems plausible."

"But is he actually sleeping with these girls? Still seems shady as hell."

"...Hey." Shido glared at the whispered accusations, and his classmates burst out in what sounded like forced laughter. He let out an exasperated sigh. "Give me a break. You're basically just making stuff up over there..."

Then he turned to the girls and tried to be upbeat. "Okay, gang. I was planning to leave early today anyway, so how about we all head home together?"

Tohka's eyes widened in surprise. "Mm? We're going already?"

"Yeah. I've already done what I came to do," he said. "I'll come get you once homeroom is over, so how about you wait a bit in the teachers' room?"

"Mm... Fine. If you say so, Shido," Tohka agreed obediently.

"Thanks. See you—" Shido placed a hand on Tohka's shoulder and then frowned. He thought he saw some kind of light flashing outside the classroom window.

But this moment of confusion was pushed aside by Tohka crying out and the clamoring of the classmates around them.

"Huh...?!"

"What's wrong—?" Shido turned his gaze from the window to Tohka and stopped abruptly.

Which was only natural. Because the seams of Tohka's clothes were gently pulling apart under Shido's hand.

"Wh-what are you doing, Shido?!" Tohka turned bright red and curled up on the spot to try and hide her exposed shoulders.

"Hey! What are you up to, Itsuka?!"

"Finally showing your true face, you predator!"

"Huh? What?"

Shido had no idea what was even happening. Tohka's clothes fell apart the moment he touched them? That wasn't—

But then one possibility popped up in Shido's mind. The flash of light outside the window. *What if that was—?*

"No way... Natsumi?!" he said under his breath, and looked toward the window once more.

Yes. The Spirit Natsumi and her Angel, which could change matter into whatever form she wished. She could definitely have done this. Meaning that it wasn't that the seams had come apart; the clothing had simply been turned into loose pieces of fabric. The moment he realized this, Shido started moving toward the window.

But this apparently looked like a criminal fleeing the scene to the people in his class. Ai-Mai-Mii formed a wall in front of him to block his path.

"Hang on there a minute, mister!"

"Where do you think you're going after wronging an innocent girl?!"

"Caught red-handed! You're not going anywhere!"

"Th-that's not what this is!" he cried. "Please get out of my way!"

But no matter what he said, Ai-Mai-Mii showed no signs of budging. They crossed their arms firmly in front of him.

"Ngh!"

Left with no other choice, Shido was about to push them aside when he saw another flash outside the window, and the uniforms the girls were wearing fell apart, exposing their soft, fair skin.

"Eek! Eeeeeaaaaaaah?!"

"Wh-what is going oooooooon?!"

"Kasaaaaap?!"

The threesome shrieked and crouched down to hide themselves. A shiver of fear ran through the classroom.

"Y-you've gone too far, Itsuka!" Tonomachi grabbed Shido's shoulders to try and stop him. But whatever accusations flew at him, there was nothing Shido could actually do.

"No, I didn't—"

A bright spot appeared outside the window for the third time. It was Tonomachi's turn to lose his clothes.

"Noooooo?!" he shouted, and fell backward onto the floor. In a moment of impossibly good fortune, a scrap of his undone outfit perfectly hid his crotch. It was a miracle.

"H-hey, what the hell?!"

"His clothes just...?!"

"One touch from Itsuka, and you're naked?!"

"No, seriously, I—" Shido tried to plead his case, and now, before his very eyes, Tama was stripped of her clothing.

"Waaahyaaaah?!" She hid her chest with the attendance ledger as she turned resentful eyes on Shido. "Wh-what are you doing, Itsuka?! Now I'll have to ask you to take responsibility for this and marry me!"

"But I didn't even touch you, though?!" He protested the grievous false charge, but it appeared that the damage had been done.

"No way! With just his eyes?!"

"How is that possible? Is he a magician?!"

"Oh, come on!" Shido scratched at his head and put his blazer over Tohka's shoulders. "Gang! It's Natsumi! We're going home!"

"...!"

Natsumi's name told Tohka, Origami, Kaguya, and Yuzuru everything they needed to know. They nodded firmly and left the classroom together with Shido.

"You stop right there, Itsukaaaaaaaaa!"

"The next time we see you, you're in for iiiiiiiit!"

"I'll strip you butt naked!"

The angry roars of Ai-Mai-Mii at his back, Shido slipped out into the hallway.

"We were in some real trouble there." Shido sighed heavily after parting ways with Origami as he trudged along the road to his own home with the miniature Spirits.

"You okay, Shido?" Tohka looked at him worriedly, wearing his blazer with the sleeves rolled up.

Shido gently caressed her face as he smiled to try and reassure her.

But nothing about the situation had been resolved. He'd gotten in touch with Kotori immediately after the incident in the classroom and had her search the places where Natsumi might have been, but they hadn't found anything that even resembled a clue. If this malicious harassment continued, Shido's reputation was as good as dead.

Of course, outside that threat, he couldn't ignore the fact that Tohka and the other girls had been put in an untenable situation. When Shido looked at them, he clenched his fists as a new resolve welled up within him.

"We have to find Natsumi right away," he declared.

"Keh-keh, a truth indeed," Kaguya agreed. "Having set us in such a form as this, we must have her pay with her very life."

Yuzuru nodded. "Assent. We cannot overlook this."

"Just so you know, we're not gonna do anything extreme, okay?" Shido said with a smile, as they rounded the corner and stood in front of the Itsuka house.

However.

"Hmm?" He tilted his head to one side, confused. His house was not where he remembered it being.

Actually, it would have been more correct to say that there was a different building where his house should have been. Shaped almost like a castle, it was very out of place in this quiet residential area.

"Ooh! It's Dream Park!" Tohka cried out excitedly.

Yes. For some reason, Shido's house had been transformed into a perfect copy of the hotel with "short stays" on the outskirts of town.

"Th-this…" For a few seconds, he was baffled as to how this could have happened, but the answer quickly dawned on him. There was exactly one Spirit who could do something like this.

"Natsumi," he said, a bead of sweat trickling down his cheek, and touched a finger to his earpiece. "Hey, Kotori. Kotori!"

Before too long, he heard Kotori's voice. *"What's up? If you're after Natsumi's location, we still—"*

"No, it's not that. You wanna pop your head out the window a sec?"

"Huh?"

A few seconds later, Kotori stuck her head out of one of the windows of the hotel.

"*Wh-what the—?! Our house is...?!*" Kotori cried out, stunned. Apparently, it was only the exterior that was different.

"Yeah," he said. "Probably Natsumi's work."

"*Tch! That power of hers is a real nuisance. Well, the inside's the same, so get in here.*"

"R-right." Shido nodded and moved toward the house-slash-hotel. However, it was then that the housewives chatting by the side of the road called out to him.

"My! If it isn't Shido Itsuka! Who on earth are all these children...?"

"Huh?! O-oh, they're just..."

"Oh my? Was...was this building always here?"

"Shido? Were you trying to take these girls in there?"

"Whaaat?! Oh my—! Police! Poliiiiice!"

"Eeep?!" Shido couldn't afford to be arrested now of all times. He grabbed the girls and fled the scene.

Chapter 7
Headhunting

The air in the conference room at the UK head office of DEM Industries was stifling. It was almost palpably viscous. A single breath filled the lungs with a heavy, agonizing muddiness. If an outsider was abruptly tossed into the room, they might have fallen into serious respiratory distress.

The men gathered there had several traits in common. They were all British, for one. They were all DEM executives, for another. And every last one of them had their arms wrapped in plaster and bandages.

"Goddammit!" A bespectacled executive in the prime of his life broke the silence. Roger Murdock.

"This is acceptable to you?! Even after he does *this* to us, you stay silent?" he shouted angrily, and indicated his right arm, suspended in a sling like everyone else's. The arm that had been cut off at the last board meeting.

These executives had demanded the dismissal of the DEM Industries managing director a few days earlier and been overruled with physical violence.

The severed arms had been neatly reconnected by medical Realizers, and the men could once again move their fingertips of their own volition. But the sight of their own arms vanishing instantly had not faded from their memories, and not one of them had yet worked up the nerve to remove his cast.

"Talk's all well and good, but..." A bearded man—Simpson—turned his eyes toward Murdock. There was a hint of fear and what looked to be censure in his gaze.

But Simpson wasn't the only one blaming Murdock. Although none of the others in the conference room were saying it out loud, it was easy to imagine they all felt something quite similar.

It would have been stranger if they didn't blame him. After all, the reason they lost their arms—the request for Westcott's dismissal—had been part of a plan devised by Murdock.

Given that Westcott had created the revolutionary Realizer technology and launched the company known as DEM Industries, his achievements were immeasurable. But this overbearing, arrogant man wielded absolute power without even once bothering to consider the external impacts of his actions. It had gotten to the point where he was nothing more than a thorn in the side of the current DEM board of directors.

And then the news had come of his outrageous actions in Japan.

As a result of nearly destroying DEM's Japanese branch buildings No. 1 and 2, along with several connected facilities, Westcott had caused the death or injury of a number of Wizards. It had been the perfect opportunity to question his leadership.

However, *this* had been the result of that defiant act.

Simpson shook his head, a note of resignation bleeding into his expression.

"This has made me realize all over again: The man is a monster. He's a different breed. His thinking, his values, the ability to implement them—all of it. We were fools to have had that fleeting dream of unseating him."

Murdock clenched his left hand into a fist and returned Simpson's gaze. "All the more so, then. I intend to have him receive his just desserts."

The executives let out a short sigh. Probably because they took this as a bluff on Murdock's part.

"Just desserts, hmm?" Simpson said, shrugging. "And what exactly are you suggesting we do?"

But Murdock most certainly did not mean his statement as a bluff or show of courage. He glared at the executives lined up there before speaking again.

"MD Westcott is in Japan right now. Some nonsense about a place with an unbelievably high frequency of Spirit appearances."

"And so?" Simpson demanded. "What of it?"

"I'm concerned," Murdock replied. "*If* he was, for instance, to be caught up in an accident or a spacequake, it would be quite a terrible loss."

"...!"

The executives collectively gasped at the meaningful stress Murdock placed on the word *if.*

"Murdock, you can't actually mean...," Simpson said with trepidation.

It wasn't only him. The rest of the room understood only too well that Murdock was insinuating they assassinate Westcott.

"..."

Silence filled the conference room. The executives let their eyes roam, as if trying to gauge the reactions of their fellows.

That said, however, it was very easy to see that their hesitation came not from the idea of taking a human life. If they had such admirable ideals, they wouldn't have been sitting on the DEM board.

What they struggled with was simply fear. They were afraid of the retribution that Westcott would no doubt subject them to in the event that the assassination failed.

However, after some length of time had passed, one of the executives spoke up. "Yes, indeed. It's worrying. Very concerning."

These carefully chosen words were nothing more than a vote in favor of Murdock's proposal.

"Mm, very true. You're quite right."

One after the other, the board members expressed their concern for Westcott until eventually, every one of them had voiced their agreement with Murdock.

The corners of Murdock's mouth turned up. *All according to plan.*

In the past, some directors might not have been on board with

Murdock's proposal. But the new experience of having their arms sliced off at a meeting was still fresh in their memories and had changed their thinking.

In other words, the fear of potentially having to continue going along with the monstrous Westcott had won out over their fear of going against him. But although Murdock had gotten his consensus, plenty of issues remained.

"But"—Simpson paused, looking troubled—"is there a means of doing *that*, then, I wonder."

It was an obvious question. While DEM had used such methods on rare occasions to eliminate problems for which no peaceful resolution could be foreseen, the power implemented in such cases was none other than the Wizards of the second enforcement division. But…

"The Wizards of the second enforcement division are all with Westcott," he said. "No matter what we try to tempt them with, it's unlikely that they'll come over to our side."

A gray-haired executive nodded at Simpson's words. "And even supposing we earn that division's cooperation, *she* is always by Westcott's side."

She. The word alone made the executives swallow hard.

Ellen M. Mathers. Westcott's right hand and the very person who had deprived Murdock and the other executives of their arms.

A Wizard boasting the greatest power at DEM—no, of all humanity. As long as she stood with Westcott, they could send all the assassins they wanted, but they would only meet a grisly fate.

Murdock hadn't forgotten about her in his attempt to take out Westcott, however. He twisted his lips up in a sneer.

"Did you know that there are currently several DEM satellites in orbit?" he asked, seemingly out of nowhere.

"What?" Simpson furrowed his brow, openly questioning the abrupt change in subject.

But Murdock ignored him and continued. "To be precise, there are twenty-three. Of these, eight have been decommissioned and are awaiting disposal."

"Now stop just a second. I can't see what this has to do with anything. Why are you suddenly talking about satellites?"

The directors all looked perplexed. Apparently, not one of them had yet caught onto his plan, even though he had laid it out so clearly. Murdock smiled boldly. "We drop the decommissioned satellite DSA-IV on the city of Tengu."

"...!"

The directors gasped as one.

Before long, Simpson shook his head. "Just when I was wondering what you were on about... Do you really think that's possible? I'm sure you are well aware the Earth has an atmosphere. Artificial satellites normally burn up before they ever reach the ground. Even assuming there would be something left to hit the ground after reentry, it would be utterly impossible to have it fall on MD Westcott's exact position."

"Is that really the case?" Murdoch asked in reply.

"What?" Simpson frowned doubtfully.

"Allow me to explain." Murdock grinned and continued. "First..."

As he spoke, he saw the faces of the directors change. Hearing Murdock's proposal, they realized for the first time that this plan was not the stuff of mere dreams.

"And that's about it," he said. "Any questions?"

One of the directors spoke up, sweat beading on his forehead. "I see. In that case, it might be feasible. But I wonder if this method won't also produce quite significant damage to the city of Tengu."

"Exactly! We might be able to strike Westcott down, but the blowback will be too great! Even assuming this does succeed, how do you intend to explain it to the world?!" A bald man raised his voice in agreement.

But this reaction was well within what Murdock had been expecting. He nodded calmly as he replied, "We dispatch an airship to Tengu at the specified time, deploy a constant Territory, and conceal the existence of the satellite from the measurement devices on the ground. And then we sound a spacequake alarm and have the residents in the area evacuate. Of course, given that the shelters were built with spacequakes in mind, we don't know how much they will be able to withstand."

"Wha...?!" came a voice in protest.

"What a tragedy. Tengu in the Tokyo Metropolitan Area will be struck by a large-scale spacequake for the first time in thirty years. And one so powerful that the shelters themselves are blown away."

Murdock sighed and continued theatrically.

"In an even greater tragedy, our very own MD was in the city at the time. Aah, how heartbreaking! Having such a genius torn away from us so young is a grave loss for DEM. But we cannot grieve forever. Shall we not carry on as he would have wanted and take DEM to even greater heights?"

Murdock finished with a flourish, and the directors grew pale as they stared at him.

However, no matter how much time passed, not a single one of them spoke up in objection to the inhumanity of the plan.

"Aaah."

November 1. Shido was exhausted.

Although he'd managed to somehow avoid being picked up by the police after that encounter with his neighbors, Natsumi's harassment had continued unchecked.

If he went out for a bit to do the shopping, the very regular clothes he was wearing would turn into a studded leather jacket and a single pair of briefs so that he suddenly looked like a total degenerate. Or a group of random strangers in his immediate vicinity would change into young naked girls, leading to another near miss with the police. And when he returned home, his house would be neon pink and look like a sleazy sex club. He couldn't even count the number of times he would have been socially obliterated if Ratatoskr hadn't been there to provide support.

"Shido, you seem sad. You okay?" Tohka peered at his face anxiously.

When he looked up, he saw it wasn't just Tohka; Yoshino, the Yamai sisters, Miku, and even Kotori were all staring at Shido in concern (the latter from behind a pillar).

He shook his head to reassure the girls and let out a sigh. This whole situation was hardest for Tohka and the others—after all, they been turned into little kids—and yet here he was feeling sorry for himself. It was shameful.

"Yeah, I'm okay," he said. "Sorry, gang."

"Mm. Yeah? As long as you're okay, then!" Tohka beamed at him, looking entirely relieved, and he somehow felt like he could relate to all those fathers with daughters. He gently patted her head.

While it was true that Natsumi's harassment grew more malicious with each passing day, that same harassment might have been the chance he'd been looking for.

At the very least, Shido would have had to be within range of Haniel when Natsumi altered his clothes or his surroundings. Naturally, since she herself could change into anything, it would be hard to actually identify her, but as a result of analyzing the Spirit signals over the last few days, a pattern was finally becoming clear. Reine and the rest of the Ratatoskr analysts were currently casting a net around the Itsuka house with the idea that in the not-too-distant future, they would be able to capture Natsumi.

In fact, what Shido should have actually been worried about was that Natsumi would have her fill of torturing him or get bored and abscond off somewhere.

And then he gasped.

"...!"

He'd seen something flash outside the window. The same light he'd seen any number of times since this all started: the sign of Haniel's transformation ability being activated.

He watched as the interior of the Itsuka house and the girls in front of him all flashed with a faint glow.

"Wha…?!" He stared in stunned disbelief.

Everything was entirely different from what it had been only seconds earlier. Instead of their casual shirts and skirts and pants, the girls were now wearing leotards and fishnet tights—bunny-girl costumes. The shapes of the ears on each of their heads and the tails attached to the bottoms of each of their leotards were different, though. Tohka was a dog, Kotori a cat, Yoshino a rabbit, the Yamais monkeys, and Miku was a cow.

Naturally, these were extremely suggestive outfits, and the girls were all children at the moment. The scene practically reeked of criminal activity.

But that wasn't all.

Haniel's power had also transformed the familiar Itsuka living room so that enormous cages now enclosed Tohka and the other girls, like they were animals in a zoo. On top of that, Shido himself was now wearing a gaudy and over-the-top outfit, the sort of thing a nobleman out of a manga might wear, and his hand gripped a leather whip.

Naturally, the walls of the house had been stripped away, revealing this inner sanctum to the world at large. Sitting neatly above the cages was a sign that read, MY OWN PERSONAL ZOO.

"Wh-what's going on?!"

"A-ahhh…"

Tohka and the other girls turned beet red and crouched down to cover themselves.

"Halt!" Kaguya alone barked her displeasure. "Why are we the only ones who are simian?!"

Perhaps surprised at the sudden sight, the assembled members of the neighborhood turned their eyes toward "My Own Personal Zoo" and began to whisper or call in reports to the police. Shido pretended not to see them as he placed a hand on his earpiece.

"Reine!" he cried desperately.

"*…Mm-hmm, I know. There it is. Natsumi's signal.*"

"Really? Where is she now?!"

"*…About a kilometer from where you are now. In a building on the shopping street.*"

"A kilometer," Shido murmured as he turned his face toward the

(former location of the) window where he had seen the light. "She's doing it from that far away."

"Shido." Kotori looked at him with serious eyes, no doubt guessing at Reine's response from his reaction, and nodded firmly.

"Okay. Let's go, gang!" Shido called.

The whole scene had to have been incredibly surreal to those witnessing it from the outside, but he did his best not to pay any mind to that.

"Heh-heh. Ha-ha… Ah-ha-ha-ha-ha-ha-ha-ha!" Natsumi fell down laughing, clutching her stomach, as she watched Shido panic and shout from her perch in the distance.

She was a beautiful woman in her midtwenties, clad in a witchlike costume. Long, slender limbs; pretty face; a body hot in all the right ways, enough to make a professional model turn away in shame. Writhing and twisting in delight, she laughed and laughed until her eyes teared up.

Natsumi was on top of a building under construction about a kilometer away from the Itsuka house. She had turned part of the steel frame into a massive telescope and was happily peering through it to watch Shido's reaction.

"Aah, hilarious. Perfect," Natsumi said, and her gaze sharpened abruptly. "After all, there's no way I could let him go on and live his happy little life after he humiliated me like that."

Yes, a few days earlier, this boy, this Shido Itsuka had exposed Natsumi's deepest, darkest secret.

Sniffing indignantly, she turned the broom-shaped Angel in her hands, Haniel, upside down.

"Nooow…what should I change next?" Her lips twisted up in a bold smile as several new ways to torment Shido popped into her head.

The perfect trick would be one that wore down Shido's spirits and ruined him socially so that he could never show his face in public again. It might be fun to turn his clothing to rags right when he was walking by the police station, giving him a record for obscene exposure. No, if she was going to do that, then…

Natsumi pondered her plans with a particularly terrible look on her face, and then she suddenly frowned and yanked her head up.

"Something's coming…?"

For a second, she thought she was mistaken, but no, she could definitely sense someone approaching her.

"Shido couldn't have actually found me?" She clicked her tongue. It wasn't unthinkable. She had more or less figured out by now that Shido had the backing of some kind of larger organization. She couldn't deny the possibility that they'd been watching the area, even if Shido himself had no clue where she was.

"Sorry. I'm not letting you catch me now!" Natsumi stuck out her tongue at her as-yet-unseen pursuer and threw a leg over Haniel. "Hee-hee-hee-hee-hee! See ya!"

She kicked off the ground, and she and Haniel floated up into the air. She stared off into the distance, bent forward so the line of her body was parallel with the broom, and shot out into the sky.

The world around her rushed past dizzyingly fast. She felt like she was a drill powering her way through the air.

This mystery group could pin down Natsumi's location all they wanted, but their work was meaningless unless they had someone who could actually follow her at this speed. Imagining how upset and bewildered Shido's comrades no doubt were at that very moment, Natsumi giggled to herself.

Still, she took care to be extra-cautious and flew around for some time, going this way and that, until she arrived halfway up a deserted mountain.

"Mm, this is probably good enough for now."

If they were trying to set a trap for her around Shido, though, she should maybe switch things up going forward. Fortunately, there were any number of ways she could do that. Instead of transforming the things around him, she could transform herself and harass him.

Like, she could change into a girl with her clothes half torn off and tell the police, "Th-that boy, he…" to get Shido tossed in jail.

"Ha-ha-ha! But that's only the start. I have to take my time and really—"

Midsentence, Natsumi felt like someone was about to grab her heart from her chest and instinctively leaped backward.

In the next instant, light ripped into the spot where she had been standing, taking a chunk of out the earth.

No mistake here. Natsumi was under attack.

"Wha…?!"

They tailed me? At that speed?! Shock colored her face, but she was quick to replace that expression with a more daring look. She was under no obligation to disclose her surprise to her opponent.

"What? For one of Shido's pals, this is quite the hello." She snorted as she turned her eyes toward the source of the bombardment—up.

The person floating there slowly descended to the ground, staring at Natsumi with cold eyes the whole time.

What appeared to be a girl was completely clad in platinum armor. Hair pale and blond enough to shock a person awake, blue eyes. Though she had doll-like features, the air emanating from her was not the ephemeral aura of a sweet young maiden, but rather that of a powerful warrior.

"I must regretfully inform you, I am no 'pal' of Shido Itsuka," she said coolly.

"Hmm? You're not?" Natsumi frowned. "So then you're AST? Well, either way. What do you want?"

"I believe that's obvious," the attacker replied as she drew the enormous sword sheathed on her back. "Witch. I have come to hunt you."

The Spirit, Witch, gaped for a moment before breaking out into giggles. "Mm-hmm? I think you'll have some trouble there. And I don't really care for this 'Witch' label. Mind calling me Natsumi?" Witch—Natsumi—said with a shrug.

From the look on her face and the way she moved, she didn't appear to be particularly on guard against Ellen. Perhaps it was merely an act to hide her agitation. Or maybe she really did believe that she couldn't be beaten. If it was the latter, she was severely underestimating Ellen.

Ellen arched an annoyed eyebrow. "I won't know if I'll have 'trouble' until I try."

"Hmph." Natsumi smirked and turned what appeared to be a broom toward Ellen.

She'd seen mention of it in the reports. Haniel, the Angel with the power to transform its target into any form desired.

This was indeed an irksome ability. But no match for Ellen. She readied her high-output laser blade Caledfwlch in her right hand.

As the two women glared at each other, several other DEM Wizards dropped down from the sky and took up position behind Ellen. They had also been chasing Witch—aka Natsumi. It seemed they had only now finally caught up with them.

Actually, it was more accurate to say that they had come here following Ellen's signal. If they had been chasing after Natsumi on their own, they would no doubt have lost her entirely.

"You're late," Ellen said, her eyes still firmly focused on Natsumi, and the Wizards gasped audibly.

"Apologies, Ellen!"

"At that speed, we simply…"

Ellen let out a short sigh at this predictable response. They were DEM Wizards. They should have been far more skillful than the average Wizard. And yet *this* was what she had to work with. Ellen keenly felt the tremendous loss of Mana Takamiya and Jessica Bailey when dealing with a bunch of Wizards like this.

"I see. Ike's words do make a kind of sense, then," she said to herself, stroking her stomach, where she still had a large scar from a recent attack. Even if none of them could challenge Ellen on their own, if she had at least one person capable of taking on a supporting role for her, it would significantly increase the chances of success for their mission.

"Executive Leader Mathers, is there something…?" one of the Wizards asked tentatively.

"It's nothing," Ellen said, her tone curt. "Please focus on the battle."

"Yes, ma'am!"

The Wizards drew their weapons as one and turned harsh eyes on Natsumi.

Natsumi shrugged, not the least bit frightened by this show of power. "Whaaaat? Is that maybe why you're so confident?" she said in an open challenge. "You think you can beat me because you've got a whole gang against little old me?"

Ellen's cheek twitched. "No. You needn't worry on that point. I will not disappoint you."

"Oh, really? Well, I don't care either way!" Natsumi shouted, as she thrust Haniel out.

A magical light of Spirit power and a fierce wind shot forward to assault Ellen and her Wizards.

"—"

But Ellen kicked off the ground with a slight sniff as she manipulated her Territory and flew up into the sky. The Wizards behind her also scattered in all directions to avoid Natsumi's attack.

"You...!"

The Wizards fired micro missiles at the Spirit on the ground. The lethal projectiles cloaked in regenerative magic closed in on her, trailing white smoke through the sky.

"Hmm, hmmm!"

But even a hail of powerful missiles couldn't wipe the bold smile from Natsumi's face. She slammed the end of her broom to the ground and called out once more.

"Haniel!"

The other end of the Angel—the broom part—opened into a circle, and the mirror at its center emitted a dazzling light.

"Ngh...?!"

The Wizards quickly realized that this was no clever trick meant to blind them or anything of the like. The moment the light radiating from Haniel's mirror touched them, the menacing missiles turned into lollipops, chocolate bars, and other tasty treats.

"Wha…?!"

The Wizards cried out in confusion as the treats hit the ground and bounced up again with a silly *boing*. A sweet scent wafted through the air.

"Oh, what's this? Sweet presents for me? How delightful!" Natsumi giggled and brandished Haniel again. "Well, I'll have to give you a little something in return. Haniel!"

The Angel shone once more, and a brilliant radiance covered the area.

"…?" Ellen furrowed her brow slightly at the curious sensation that came over her. She wasn't crouched over, and yet she felt like her point of view had gotten somewhat lower.

The Wizards deployed around her cried out here and there.

"Wh-whoa?!"

"What the…?!"

Ellen cautiously shifted only her eyes to confirm what had happened. What she found were several small children she had never seen before.

No. That wasn't right. When she really looked at them, she realized that these children had the features of her subordinates. Most likely, the power of Haniel had changed them into children.

Ellen dropped her gaze to her left hand, the one not holding her laser blade. Perhaps it was only obvious at this point, but the hand she saw was much smaller than she remembered it being. It seemed that, just like the other Wizards, Ellen had been smallified. Her wiring suit had shrunk along with her body, but her CR unit was still its original size, leaving her slightly unbalanced.

"Ha-ha-ha-ha-ha-ha-ha-ha! You're way cuter like this, y'know?" Natsumi doubled over in laughter.

"The battle ith not over," Ellen told her.

"Whaaat?" Natsumi grinned up at her. "What exactly can you do in that teensy tiny body? Be a good girl and go home to your mommy. Heh-heh-heh-heh-heh!"

"…" Ellen quietly narrowed her eyes. She issued commands in

her mind to operate her Territory, scanned her body, and checked her own status to instantly grasp the amount of muscle she had, her bone density, metabolism, nervous system, and other functions. And indeed, all her abilities appeared to have diminished. Even the power to move her tongue had regressed, it seemed; she was unable to speak properly. This transformation ability was a truly irritating power.

However.

"Thith 'teenthy tiny' body ith enough to kill you," Ellen said with a lisp, as she readjusted her grip on the hilt of Caledfwlch, kicked at the ground, and charged Natsumi.

"Huh?" Caught off guard, Natsumi let out a dumbfounded cry, and her eyes flew open in surprise.

Ellen swung Caledfwlch.

"What? Huh...?!" Natsumi squeezed the cry from her throat, eyes wide open.

She couldn't understand what had happened.

She'd used Haniel to throttle her opponent's power like always. She'd made the Wizards regress and reduced their overall abilities by half. And these Wizards were nobodies to start with anyway, with no hope against the Spirit Natsumi. Her magic should have settled everything quite neatly.

Despite all this, however, one of them was swinging her sword at Natsumi.

"Whu—? Ah..."

This had never happened before.

This girl Ellen made her shining sword flash, and Natsumi felt something like a wave of heat blooming from her chest to her stomach as she went flying backward.

Natsumi pressed a hand to her stomach and then slowly raised it up before her somehow-hazy eyes. Her hand had an impossible amount of blood on it.

"Eeep!" The instant she saw this, an intense and still somehow-unreal pain danced across every nerve in her body.

It hurts. Ow-ow-ow-ow-ow. It hurts. Owowowowowowowow! "Ah. Aaaaaaaaaaah?!" She'd never felt pain on this level before. It was like thousands of sharp needles stabbing into her. Her consciousness was fading, her field of vision blurred. But the unrelenting violence of the pain would not allow her to pass out. Hellish waves lapped at her nerve endings ceaselessly.

"Ungh. This... What...?"

A single blow from Ellen's blade of light had sliced through Natsumi's Astral Dress and deep into her body. Even after she figured out what had happened, Natsumi still couldn't process it fully.

But whether she accepted it or not, the reality of the situation was unchanged. From where she lay on the ground, she could see Ellen wielding her sword of light.

"I thee. I have been weakened. To think that I could mith your vitalth when attacking from closh range," Ellen said, before her body began to glow and she returned to her original appearance of a woman of about eighteen.

Most likely, the transformation of any low-priority targets had been undone when Natsumi was injured. She was still able to maintain the changes to her own body.

"Oh my, I've returned to normal, hmm?" Ellen opened and closed her left hand as though checking in on her body before dropping her gaze to Natsumi once more. "Now then, what shall we do? I could capture you alive, or I could kill you and take just the Sefirah."

"...!" Natsumi desperately tried to speak. "H-helb... I...dond... wanna diiieee..."

"It doesn't matter to me either way, but I do think that that option would increase suffering for you," Ellen said, as the other Wizards gathered around her, their transformations similarly undone.

"Executive Leader. What shall we do?" one of them asked.

"We'll let her live and take her with us. I doubt she'll be able to do

much of anything with this injury." Ellen adjusted her grip on the hilt of her sword once more. "But it appears that she possesses a troublesome power, so for safety's sake, I'll take off her limbs."

"Eeep?!" Natsumi gasped, and tried to scramble away from Ellen. But she didn't have the strength left to actually move.

Ellen slowly raised her sword. "It will be over soon. Please don't die while I work," she said without any emotion in her voice as she prepared to bring down the blade.

"—!!" Natsumi automatically closed her eyes and gritted her teeth in anticipation of the even more excruciating pain to come.

Right arm? Left arm? Right leg? Or maybe the left...? There was no pain yet. She was too afraid to even open her eyes or move her fingertips to check which limbs she still had left.

However.

"Wha...?"

Natsumi heard the faintest hint of surprise in Ellen's voice, and she timidly, nervously opened her eyes.

"Huh?" she cried out in stunned amazement at the unexpected sight before her.

It was the back of a small girl clad in a glowing Astral Dress, brandishing a sword about as big as she was, defending Natsumi from Ellen's attack.

Natsumi immediately realized she'd seen this girl before. Tohka Yatogami. One of the girls Natsumi had turned into a child the other day.

"Haaah!" With a determined cry, Tohka swung her massive blade.

Instead of counterattacking, Ellen leaped back to put some distance between them.

Tohka glared at Ellen, not letting her guard down. "Are you okay?!" she shouted to Natsumi.

"Wh-why are you...? What are you...?" Natsumi stammered, and then she heard a daring song somewhere nearby.

At the same time, the temperature dropped abruptly, and the moisture in the air started to freeze with a *crackle*. Frost fell and became something like an invisible wall blanketing the trees and ground and the Wizards.

"Ngh?!"

"My Territory's freezing?!"

"Not good! Release your Territory, then redeploy and retreat to the sky!"

The Wizards released their freezing Territories for the merest of instants.

"Keh-keh-keh! A sagacious strategy! Well, in the normal course of events, it would be correct!"

"Misfortune. But given that we are here, I am forced to say that this is a poor move."

A heartbeat before the Wizards could redeploy their Territories, derisive yet childish voices called out, accompanied by an exceptionally powerful wind that ripped through the area and easily sent the defenseless Wizards flying.

"Wh-whoa?!"

"Keh-kah-kah-kah! Clumsy! Amateurs!"

"Sneer. Pathetic."

Bright laughter and a monotone voice echoed through the air as identical twins came down to stand on the ground. The Yamai sisters. They had also been turned into children because of Natsumi's power.

"...?!" The confusion on Natsumi's face now was of a different type. She didn't understand. Why, after she had hurt them in all kinds of ways, would they come to her aid now?

"Natsumi!"

A sudden call interrupted her jumbled thoughts, and Shido Itsuka appeared from behind and knelt down beside her.

"You're bleeding!" he cried. "Are you okay?!"

"Shi...do...?"

Even you?

She couldn't say the words out loud. Perhaps because she had lost too much blood, the strength was draining from her body.

"Ngh." He gritted his teeth. "We'll get you fixed up in no time!"

"Do you believe I would allow that?" Ellen said. Of all the Wizards the Yamais had knocked flying, she was the only one who'd maintained her Territory and avoided it freezing by increasing the magic concentration. "Princess, Berserk, and the cold air is Hermit? And this song... It would appear that Diva is hiding somewhere nearby. I see. Then it would make sense that Princess was able to exchange blows with me, albeit in a surprise attack, even when her power has been diminished."

She narrowed her eyes.

"Six Spirits, five as children, and the remaining Spirit is gravely injured. Ike only told me to take stock of the situation, but it's quite a different story when conditions are this favorable."

Ellen readied her sword once more.

With nervous eyes, Shido glared at her. "You sure about that, Ellen? Your friends have all been wiped out. You're outnumbered."

"I appreciate the concern," she replied coolly. "But they were never part of the equation to begin with."

Sweat popped up on Shido's forehead. Even he could see that Ellen was vastly superior to any other Wizard out there. He might have had more people on his side, but Ellen was abnormally powerful. It was one thing if all the Spirits had been at full strength, but in this situation, they didn't have a chance of winning.

Still, he licked his lips and called out, "Yeah? Then we'll go ahead and take full advantage of our numbers. Miku!"

The song drifting through the air around them changed.

In contrast with the previous rousing March, this tune had a bewitching charm, graceful and delicate, almost as if the music notes were slipping into their very minds.

"Whatever you try, it's pointless," Ellen told him. "That sort of thing doesn't—"

"Yeah, wouldn't work, right?" Shido grinned. "Not on *you*."

"What did you say?" Ellen furrowed her brow dubiously just as the defeated Wizards roused themselves clumsily, like marionettes, and began to swarm Ellen.

"Tch!" Ellen clicked her tongue in annoyance and took a firm step with one foot. The invisible wall deployed around her swelled outward and stopped the movement of the zombie Wizards swarming her.

Shido placed a hand on his ear, like this was exactly what he had expected. "Now! Kotori! Pick us up!"

Suddenly, Natsumi felt her body wrapped in a curious buoyancy.

"Wh...at...?"

"This might hurt, but just grin and bear it for a second!" Shido told her.

"Huh...?" Natsumi felt herself pulled upward and her own transformation release, and then she passed out.

"...?!"

In her living room. Origami frowned at the strange feeling that suddenly overcame her. With no warning whatsoever, her body shone faintly, and then slowly but surely, she started to grow taller and return to the form she'd had before the Spirit Natsumi turned her into a child.

"What...?"

As if to confirm this, she clenched her hands and rolled her shoulders. She couldn't find anything particularly out of place. She really had returned to normal.

"What on earth...?"

What had happened? Did Natsumi get tired of her games? Or had Shido found her and succeeded in talking her down? Had the AST managed to overpower her? Origami could think of several possible causes of the change, but whatever the real reason was, this was without a doubt good news.

She stood up.

"Ngh..."

Perhaps as an effect of suddenly returning to her original body size, her head spun a little, like she was dizzy from standing up too fast. She set a hand on the table to steady herself, and the light-headedness subsided after a few seconds.

She lifted her face again. First and foremost, she needed to clarify the situation. She had to go to Shido and ask him what had happened. And it would be a good idea to check if Tohka Yatogami and the other Spirits had also returned to normal. If they were still in child form, then the school would obviously become Origami and Shido's love nest, and no one would get in their way.

It might also have been a good idea to check in at the AST Tengu Garrison. Because she was awaiting discipline for disobeying orders, Origami couldn't take part in any missions, but she could ask her colleague Mikie and the mechanic Mildred for the latest news on the team.

At any rate, now that she'd settled on a plan, she pulled at the neck of her shirt. She had returned to her original size while wearing children's clothing, so it no longer fit her. She went into her bedroom and grabbed something to wear out of the closet. After quickly changing, Origami headed for the entryway.

But then she raised her eyebrows.

The reason was simple. She could sense someone outside her front door.

Her condo was equipped with a secure entrance, and no one could enter the building without the permission of a resident. It was hard to imagine it was a delivery or a salesperson. In which case…

"…"

Silently, Origami pressed against a wall and kept her eyes on the front door as she pulled a small automatic weapon from a leg holster.

Soon, she heard a faint *click*, and the door was yanked open. Several men stepped inside, but they had barely crossed the threshold when the wire strung across the door was tripped and a spray of tear gas shot out at them.

"Ngah?!"

"Wha…? This…"

The men cried out in confusion. They probably hadn't expected a trap in a regular condominium.

Origami furrowed her brow the slightest bit. There were more of them than she'd expected. It wasn't clear that she would win if she engaged the intruders.

Making this judgment in a split second, she cut across the room and slipped out through a window. In preparation for such an eventuality, she had set up footholds on the wall of the building (without the landlord's knowledge). She moved rhythmically across these to make her way to the ground.

"She went out the window!"

"After her!"

She could hear the men's voices above. She couldn't stay here. She grabbed the shoes that she had hidden on the condo grounds (just in case), slipped them on, and started running toward the city center.

"Those men…who were they?" she murmured to herself as she fled, searching for some clue in her brain. But she couldn't think of anyone who would force their way into her house out of the blue.

While she was considering this, her phone began to vibrate in her pocket. Without slowing down, she fumbled around in her pocket and pulled her phone out to find the name RYOUKO KUSAKABE displayed on the screen. The captain of the AST squad Origami belonged to.

When she pressed the ANSWER button and put the phone to her ear, she quickly heard a familiar voice.

"Hello? Origami?"

"What?" Origami responded while running.

Ryouko gasped, perhaps guessing at the situation. *"You're not actually fleeing, are you?"*

"…How do you know that?" Origami asked briefly.

Ryouko was silent for a moment before continuing in a pained tone, like the words were hard to say. *"I need you to stay calm and listen to me. They just decided on disciplinary measures for you."*

"…!" Now it was Origami's turn to gasp.

Everything clicked into place all at once. The men who had broken into her condo were agents dispatched to arrest her. She had heard that problem subjects were taken into custody before being told about their punishment so they couldn't resist.

Last month, to protect Shido, Origami had used prohibited weaponry and mounted an attack on a DEM squad, supposedly an ally of her organization. She had been forbidden from taking part in AST missions until the matter was settled. But at the root of the incident was DEM's recklessly selfish actions, and word was that even some of the high-ranking officers were in agreement with Origami and what she had done to stop the DEM squad. *Why on earth—?*

As if guessing at her train of thought, Ryouko continued. *"The majority of officers agreed that yours should be handled as a special case. But when the ruling came down, it still called for disciplinary action. It's pretty clear that some big shot's making a power move behind the scenes."*

"DEM," Origami said flatly.

"..." Ryouko didn't respond to this, but her silence was more than answer enough. *"At any rate, I'm going to go talk to the brass. Right now—"*

"There she is! This way!"

A man appeared on the road in front of Origami, blocking her path forward. It was hard to imagine that he'd gotten around ahead of her. Most likely, there had been another unit right from the start.

"...!"

Left with no other choice, she headed onto a side street, but it turned out to be a dead end. She was out of options.

"You've really led us on quite a chase, Master Sergeant Tobiichi. Your punishment's been decided. Come with me," a man who seemed to be the squad leader said, as he stepped forward and glared at Origami.

Ignoring him, Origami examined her surroundings, moving just her eyeballs. Front, above, left, right. But she couldn't spot a route that would allow her to escape from this many people.

The squad leader snorted. "It's no use. Come quietly."

"Ngh..." Origami shot daggers at the man with her eyes when the phone in her hand began to vibrate abruptly.

Incoming call. She must have accidentally hung up on Ryouko when she was running away from these agents. No doubt Ryouko was trying to call her back now.

This might have been an opportunity to gain new information. Still glaring at the man, guard up, Origami pressed the ANSWER button without looking at the screen and pressed the phone to her ear.

"Hello? Have I reached the cellular telephone of Master Sergeant Origami Tobiichi?"

The voice she heard was not the one she'd been expecting.

"...! Ellen Mathers...?" Origami furrowed her brow as she spoke the name. Ellen. A DEM Wizard.

The man's eyebrows arched slightly at the sound of this name.

"What do you want?" Origami demanded.

"Please don't be so brusque, Master Sergeant Tobiichi," Ellen said, perhaps picking up on the hint of an edge in Origami's voice.

But Origami was about to lose her power because of DEM at that very moment. There was no way she could see them as anything but the enemy. And even before that, Origami and Ellen had very recently crossed swords at the DEM Japan office. Of course, the difference in their abilities had been crystal clear, but Origami had managed to land a hit on Ellen. There was no way Ellen thought well of Origami.

But Ellen didn't allow any hint of ill will toward Origami bleed into her voice. She continued in an extremely businesslike tone. *"Allow me to come straight to the point. Master Sergeant Tobiichi. Would you consider working under me?"*

"... Meaning?" Origami frowned suspiciously at the unexpected words.

"Exactly what it sounds like," Ellen replied. *"Would you ally with the DEM Industries second enforcement division? I promise you better working conditions in every aspect than what you enjoy currently."*

"I have no intention of helping an organization intent on harming Shido," Origami snapped.

"You can rest assured, then. Our policy for the time being is to not proactively attack Shido Itsuka."

"And you're telling me to trust you?" Origami said.

"I see." Ellen let out a short sigh. *"That is unfortunate. However, are you certain? It appears that you've been placed in quite the difficult*

situation. If you are apprehended now, you will permanently lose the ability to challenge the Spirits."

"...!" Origami narrowed her eyes sharply. Ellen knew exactly what was happening right now.

Instantly, the threads all came together. She understood the reason why DEM had intervened to ensure disciplinary measures for Origami.

"You don't hold a grudge against me for hurting you?" she asked.

"I won't say that I bear you no ill will. But currently, my desire for a useful subordinate is winning out over that trivial feeling. I need someone strong enough to hurt me."

"..."

Although Origami remained silent and Ellen had no way of seeing the look on her face, Ellen continued as if she could read Origami's thoughts.

"DEM Industries has any number of CR units with performance that far surpasses those that are provided to the various nations of the world. Do you not wish to at last allow your parents to rest in peace?"

"...!"

Ellen had apparently looked into Origami's past as well.

She sighed unhappily. But what Ellen said next stopped Origami from voicing her displeasure.

"Five years ago, a large fire enveloped Tengu's Nanko district. Multiple Spirit signals were confirmed on the scene at the time. Naturally, this is classified DEM information, but if you become a Wizard with the second enforcement division, I would be amenable to disclosing it to you."

"Wha—?" Origami's eyes flew open.

Multiple Spirit signals. This backed up what Shido had told her. Shido's little sister, Efreet, Kotori Itsuka. Origami had pursued this flame Spirit to get revenge for her parents. But Shido told her then that another Spirit had been there at the time and that Kotori wasn't responsible for the death of Origami's parents.

"What are you jabbering about?!" the man standing in front of

Origami called out in a disgruntled voice with impeccable timing, almost like he'd been signaled to act at that moment. "Enough. Grab her!"

The other men closed in to surround Origami.

"Ngh!" she groaned.

"Now then. What will it be, Master Sergeant Tobiichi?"

"…" After a few seconds of silence, Origami voiced her decision. "Fine. Give me power."

An instant later…

"Ngh?!"

"Hrk! Ah!"

…the men who were about to arrest Origami cried out in agony and began to drop to the ground one after the other.

"What…?" Origami frowned as a girl with Nordic blond hair and a phone pressed to her ear strolled forward from behind the line of fallen men.

She extended a hand toward Origami. From in front of her and over the phone, Origami heard Ellen Mathers's voice.

"Welcome to DEM Industries."

Chapter 8
Makeup

"So Natsumi's awake?!" Shido cried out, as he threw open the door.

A room was set up like the bridge of *Fraxinus*, with various devices and an enormous monitor, in one corner of an underground Ratato-skr facility within the city.

"Oh, Shido. That was fast." A chair in the center of the room whirled around, and the girl sitting in it turned her face toward him. Kotori.

When Natsumi lost consciousness, Haniel's transformations were undone, and Kotori was back to looking the way Shido remembered her.

Actually, not quite exactly how he remembered her. He cocked his head dubiously to one side.

"Hmm? Kotori, what happened to your face?"

When he looked closely, he could see faint red lines on her face. Almost like she'd been scratched by a cat.

"Oh." Kotori patted her cheek. "Well, just be careful, Shido."

"...Of what?" He stared at her and then sighed. "Actually, never mind. Anyway, where's Natsumi? She's regained consciousness, right?"

"Yes." Kotori nodded. "Not too long ago. This way."

Following her prompt, Shido left the room and walked down a hall-way larger than the ones on *Fraxinus*, the soles of his shoes clacking rhythmically. He'd never been here before, but he could tell the facility had a similar structure as the one they'd used when trying to pinpoint whom Natsumi was disguised as. Ratatoskr appeared to have several of this kind of facility ready for various situations.

After Kotori and her crew had picked up Natsumi in *Fraxinus* the previous day, they'd immediately transferred her here and carried out treatment and tests. Even trying to put a positive spin on things, it was hard to say that the injury Ellen had dealt her was a superficial one, but fortunately, it was not life-threatening.

"There's the whole thing with Ellen, too," Kotori said, as she walked down the hall, glancing at Shido from time to time. "Honestly, I'd really rather hold Natsumi on *Fraxinus*. But we can't exactly bring an unsealed Spirit up there."

That was true. If a fully powered Spirit ran rampant on the airship, the isolated secure area would do little to contain her.

"In here." Kotori abruptly stopped, and Shido caught sight of a sturdy door in front of them.

And then, with a practiced movement, Kotori punched in a number on the terminal next to the door before placing her hand on the area below the number pad. There was a small *beep*, and the door slid open.

"Go ahead, Shido." She gestured him forward.

"Right…" He stepped inside and found a large space beyond the door. Several machines were arranged in the dim area, and in the center, he could see a room partitioned off with a solid glass wall. The setup was very similar to that of the isolation space Kotori had been placed in on *Fraxinus* when her powers returned.

And on the bed inside this room, a girl sat fiddling with a stuffed animal, her face twisted up grumpily.

"Natsumi," Shido said quietly.

The girl with serious bedhead, unhealthily pale skin, and limbs as skinny as sticks was sitting in a hospital gown on the bed. To Shido's eyes, Natsumi looked like a patient ravaged by a serious disease whose days were numbered.

This was a very different sight from the Spirit Natsumi, whom Shido and the others had rescued the previous day. But he knew that this figure he could see through the glass was the real Natsumi.

"I know I don't have to tell you this, but," Kotori said, flicking the stick of her Chupa Chups back and forth across her lips, "make sure you're careful. It looks like she can't use her Angel right now because Ellen did a number on her, but she's still a Spirit. And her numbers when it comes to you are extremely low."

"Yeah, I know," he said. "But we can't do anything unless I talk to her."

"Exactly." Kotori nodded firmly. "Unless Natsumi opens up to you, we won't be able to seal her Spirit powers. I won't go telling you to make her weak in the knees right here and now, but at least create some kind of opening with her. We won't get a chance like this again."

"A chance like this?" Shido repeated curiously, and Kotori shrugged in a deliberate fashion.

"Well, yeah. She's seriously hurt and can't use her power the way she normally would. On top of that, she's confined in an unfamiliar place. She might put on a show of acting tough, but she's got to be a little anxious. There's a strong possibility that your likability will increase if you can put her worries to rest."

"I hope it's as easy as that," he said. "If it were me, I'd be pretty wary."

"Mm," Kotori agreed. "But you're the hero who put his life on the line to save her. I don't think she'll be too mean to you."

"Fingers crossed." Shido took a deep breath. "I'm going in."

He put a hand on the entrance to the glass-partitioned room and slowly pushed the door open. The wall, which was transparent from the outside, appeared to be an ordinary white wall when seen from the inside. In addition to the bed, the room contained some shelves and a table. There were also a number of games and toys and the like; Shido could see in them Ratatoskr's desperate efforts to try and ensure somehow that Natsumi didn't get bored.

"...!"

The moment he entered the room, Natsumi jolted where she sat on the bed.

"H-hey... Natsumi." He tried to keep a natural-ish smile on his face as he greeted her. But not only did she not return the greeting, she also started throwing the pillows and cushions from the bed, stuffed animals, and anything else she could get her hands on.

"...! Ngh...!" She grunted with the effort.

"Ah!" he yelped. "Hey! Quit that, Natsumi!"

"Do—! Lo... Ee!"

"Huh?" He frowned. He couldn't really catch what she said.

"Don't...look...at me!"

"What? Why not?" Shido tilted his head to one side, and a panda came sailing through the air to hit him smack in the face. "Umpf?!"

"...!"

But that panda was apparently the final projectile. Realizing that there was nothing left on the bed for her to throw, Natsumi turned from side to side in a panic for a second before diving under the blankets. She looked like a sniper in a ghillie suit diving under a thicket.

"Wh-what do you want?!" she demanded, glaring at him with extremely hostile eyes.

"Oh. Uh," he stammered. "I just wanted to talk."

"There's nothing to talk about! G-get out!"

"D-don't say that," he said. "How are you feeling?"

"Ungh...!" Natsumi looked away uncomfortably. After a few seconds of silence, she spoke. "Why...did you save me?"

"Why?" he parroted. "Because Ellen was about to—"

"That's not what I mean!" Natsumi shouted, cutting him off. "I—I... I pretended to be you, made your friends disappear... I've only ever been horrible to you! So why... Why would you help me?! You! And your friends, too!" She snapped out an accusing finger at him.

"Yeah." Shido crossed his arms and sighed wearily. "That was a serious mess. Not gonna lie, that was wild. You'll stop that stuff, right?"

"I'm being serious!" Natsumi cried in frustration.

Shido fell into thought for a moment, and then he quickly slapped his fist against his palm. "Oh! Right! You should apologize to everyone, too, okay?"

"Aaah! Come *on!*" Natsumi flailed her arms underneath the blankets, and dust danced up around her. Apparently, she didn't care for his response.

But he simply was at a loss when faced with the question of why he'd saved her. Scratching the back of his head, he replied, "I don't know what to tell you. Seeing you in a situation like that, what else could I do but help?"

"Do—! Don't give me that!" she cried. "There's no way you'd just help for no reason! Spit it out! What's your objective here? Exactly what kind of calculation leads to you saving the very person who's been tormenting you?!"

"No, it's just…" Shido scratched his head. "You know. It's true that you did do a fair bit of damage. But I mean, that's just how it goes with Spirits, you know? Look. Remember Tohka and Yoshino? Maybe you know this already, but they're Spirits just like you. And to be honest, they almost killed me a bunch of times."

"K-killed you?" Natsumi looked up at him.

"Yeah." He nodded. "I got hit with this beam out of the blue and almost got frozen with the entire city, too."

"H-huh?!" Now she gaped at him.

"I was for real this close to getting eaten, and oh!" he cried in sudden remembrance. "This one time, I nearly got burnt to a crisp!"

"Wait… What?" Her jaw dropped.

"And there was the time I was attacked by a typhoon and knocked flying," he said, continuing. "Oh! More recently, everyone in town got brainwashed, and they all came after me. *That* situation was seriously dicey."

"…" From a gap in the blanket, Natsumi stared at him in disbelief.

"So." Shido smiled dryly. "It's like, I can't say it was all no big deal since people did actually get hurt. But Tohka and the Spirits have all apologized and changed their ways. They've moved past it, and now they live here with us. Why couldn't you do the same thing?"

Natsumi was silent for some time before snorting indignantly. "Wh-what's that all about? You trying to sound cool or something?"

"No, not—"

Not really. He couldn't quite finish his sentence. He changed the subject instead. "Anyway, can I ask you a question?"

"…What?" Natsumi replied after a lengthy pause. The fact that she didn't immediately reject his request felt like real progress.

"I want to know why you pretended to be me and erased everyone in the first place," he said. "Why on earth would you do all that?"

"…!" Natsumi glowered at him from a gap in the blanket. "That's… It's obviously because you saw my secret that time!"

"Secret?" Shido frowned, confused.

"I—I… My actual form, of course!" Natsumi yelled with tears in her eyes.

"Huh? H-hang on a minute!" he cried. "Why would you have to do all that just because I saw you?!"

Natsumi gritted her teeth. "Why… Why?! Y-you can't be this stupid! You can tell that just by looking at me, can't you?! How could anyone be okay being seen looking so scrawny and pathetic?! And also, was it your objective to make me say it out loud?!" she shouted, very close to completely freaking out, and beat at the bed with tiny fists.

Shido didn't really get it, but him accidentally seeing her true form had apparently been a fatal attack for Natsumi.

With bloodshot eyes, Natsumi kept going in her overwrought state. "Things were getting pretty cozy the first time we met, right? You said I was beautiful, remember? But why? Because I was transformed into that woman, right?! You think you would've reacted like that if I'd looked like this then? You wouldn't have, would you? You wouldn't have been into it, would you? You might've even ignored me when I talked to you, right?!"

"I—I wouldn't—," he stammered.

"Yooouuuuuuu wouuuuuuuld, tooooooo!" she shouted, cutting him off. "Not one of the people on this side would have anything to do with me if I was me!"

"Natsumi…?" Shido felt the tone of her words change abruptly to something sad and furrowed his brow.

But she quickly narrowed her eyes again. "Anyway! I can't allow anyone who knows what I really look like to exist in this world!" She yanked the mess of blankets over her head once again. She was like a caterpillar now.

As if overwhelmed by Natsumi's intensity, Shido took a step back, her words lingering in his mind.

The gist of it was that Natsumi seriously hated the way she looked and herself in general. So she used Haniel's abilities to turn herself into her ideal woman. Essentially. In this way, she wasn't so different from the classic magical girls. Well, in Natsumi's case, though, her loathing of her true form was truly next-level. But now that he understood the core issue, there was still one thing that didn't click for him.

The problem was simple.

"Hmm." He frowned. "But, Natsumi. Are you really that disappointing the way you are?"

True, her hair was all over the place, and it would be hard to say she looked healthy, even if he was trying to be nice. But he felt like Natsumi's appearance simply didn't line up with the abuse she was hurling at herself. He could easily say she'd be plenty cute if she cleaned herself up a little.

But Natsumi greeted his question with hostile eyes. "Say whatever you want! You're not fooling me! I'm not buying a word of it!"

"No, but I'm not trying to fool you," he protested. "C'mon. Let me have a good look at your face." He walked slowly over to the bed and put a hand on the blanket Natsumi had pulled over herself.

"Nnn! Nnnnngh!" She kicked and flailed and tried to fight him off, but perhaps her struggling caused the pain from her wound to flare up, because she quickly quieted down and allowed him to peel back the blanket.

"…!"

Her face beet red, Natsumi squeezed her eyes shut and curled into a ball.

It was true that she didn't have the sensual and sultry appeal of the adult version, but if Natsumi actually put some effort into it, he was sure she'd transform into a fine little lady.

"Mm. Just like I thought," he said, as he looked her over. "Don't be so mean about yourself. You have your own charms the way you are now."

"What...?! Talking like you know anything!" Natsumi got a venomous look on her face, but Shido simply stared right back at it. She snapped her mouth shut, and her eyes swam around the room, like she wasn't entirely sure what to do.

After a brief silence, she opened her small mouth. "Really? I... I'm okay the way I am?"

"Yup. Really," Shido assented forcefully, and held out a hand toward her. "So let's go say sorry to everyone the way you are now, in your own words. It'll be okay. They'll understand. And once you apologize, you'll be able to be friends with them."

"Friends..."

"Yup."

Natsumi lowered her face hesitantly, but eventually, ever so timidly, she reached her own hand out toward Shido's.

But the moment their hands were about to touch, she flipped hers over and held up her middle finger.

"Like I'd fall for that! Stupid!" she shouted.

"Huh...?" Shido gaped at the sudden change.

"Frieeeeeends?" she sneered. "You're just saying that so you can make me a laughingstock when I fall for your stupid tricks! Like, you'll say, 'Whoa! This dodo actually thought I was serious!' And then you'll all have your big laugh, right?! You've got a sign saying 'Psych!' or something all ready, don't you?! Well, I'm onto you! I know what the score is!"

"N-no... Natsumi?" He took a step back as if overpowered by her.

But Natsumi not only didn't calm down, she actually grew even more heated.

"'This total uggo wears the face of a beautiful woman and gets all full of herself, grooooss!' That's what you're thinking, isn't it?!" she shouted accusingly. "You don't need to go opening your big fat mouth, I get it! I mean, I know better than anyone else in the world that I'm a hopeless sack of garbage! But there's nothing I can do about that, is there?! You saying I got any other options here?!"

"C-calm down, Natsumi! No one thinks tha—"

"Shut. Uuuuuuuuuuup! Guys like you who try to pretend they're all nice and kind are obviously whispering the worst stuff behind people's backs and spewing hate on social media! You probably post stuff like 'I saw this serious uggo today and almost barfed,' complete with a picture and everything! Aaaaaaaaah, just die already! Die, die, die, diiiiiiiiie! I'll ratio you! I'll screenshot everything, post it all on a massive bulletin board, and run you right out of schoooooool!"

"You're seriously up-to-date on the modern world!" Shido retorted without thinking, but now was not the time for that. He had to try and somehow soothe the raging Natsumi. "A-anyway, let's just calm down. Okay?! C'mon, take a deep breath—"

"Aaaauuuuuugh!"

But it was hopeless. Overwrought Natsumi started waving her hands, nails out, and clawed at Shido's face.

"..."

"I *told* you to be careful," Kotori said with a shrug, the same scratch marks on her own face, when Shido came out of Natsumi's room. It appeared that Natsumi had also clawed at Kotori in the same way at some point.

Shido pointedly ignored this. "Let me just ask: What's her mental state like?"

"Although it fluctuates somewhat, it's definitely not at the level where you could lock her power away."

"Of course it's not..." He stroked the still-stinging scratches on his cheeks as he turned his gaze toward the isolation room on the other side of the transparent wall. He caught sight of Natsumi panting furiously, shoulders heaving.

Maybe Shido's departure alone was enough to calm her down. Soon, she was breathing evenly again, and eventually, she jumped down from the bed to start picking up the stuffed animals and pillows she had thrown at Shido.

As far as he could tell, this was normal behavior. But to his eyes, this looked less like an act with the purpose of tidying up and absolutely like Natsumi was replenishing her ammunition to attack when someone came into the room again.

"She really has zero confidence in how she actually looks," Kotori said, troubled, a hand on her chin. "Unless we do something about this complex of hers, even if you can lock her Spirit power away, it'll just flow right back into her."

In fact, Kotori was entirely right. If he did seal Natsumi's power, she wouldn't be able to use her transformation ability. Which meant, of course, that she would have to live in her true form and not the skin of that young woman. And looking at Natsumi's current state...that was an extremely difficult ask.

"But we can't just sit and twiddle our thumbs," Kotori said. "We've got a deadline, after all."

"Deadline?" Shido parroted.

Kotori nodded as if this was self-evident. "The only reason Natsumi's quiet right now is because the damage Ellen did to her hasn't healed. Once she recovers enough to be able to use her Angel again, she'll probably escape sooner than later."

"Oh," he said. "Right. So then how long do we have?"

Kotori held up two fingers like she was making a peace sign. "According to Reine's estimates, two days at most. We have to get Natsumi to open up to us before the day after tomorrow."

"Hmm." Shido crossed his arms, frowned, and set his brain to work.

They had no time. On top of that, Natsumi was in such a state that she hated even a proper conversation with them. The first thing they needed to do was to deal with Natsumi's intense self-loathing.

"Oh!" he said, an idea popping into his head. "Hey, Kotori? I don't know how well it'd work, but how about something like this?"

"Like what?" Kotori cocked her head to one side as she arched a lone eyebrow.

Shido concisely explained his thinking.

"Mm-hmm. I get it." She put a hand on her chin and flicked up the stick of the Chupa Chups in her mouth. "Okay. We don't have any other effective possibilities. Let's give it a go. Ratatoskr will take care of the details."

"Great, thanks," Shido said. "I'll go ask everyone if they'd be down to help."

"Yes, do that. We'll carry out the plan tomorrow," she said decisively. "We'll launch a surprise attack once Natsumi's done with breakfast."

"Got it. Don't oversleep."

"Same goes for you." Kotori plucked her Chupa Chups out of her mouth and grinned. "Now. Shall we begin our date?"

"Mm…" Natsumi woke up the next morning to a delicious smell wafting through her room.

The source of the aroma soon became clear. Part of the wall had transformed into something like a table, and breakfast had been set out on top of it. Two bread rolls, bacon and eggs, soup and salad. Steam was rising from the soup, and the bacon was still sizzling. She could tell that this was not ready-made, but cooked up somewhere nearby only moments earlier.

It seemed that part of the wall opened and closed for a structure that placed meals inside the room. Lunch and supper the day before had arrived in the same way without Natsumi being aware of it.

"…"

She moved the tray from the wall to the actual table and sniffed the food on the plates warily before tentatively starting to eat.

The umami of the juicy bacon fat and the mild flavor of the eggs mixed in complicated ways in her mouth. Her cheeks started to soften into a smile, but she quickly caught herself and shook her head and the smile away.

"Dammit… Why is it so good…?" Grumbling to herself in vexation, Natsumi scarfed down the breakfast.

As she stuffed a roll loaded with jam into her mouth, she looked around the room where she was locked up once more.

Bed, table, TV. And most everything else needed for daily living. Meals and snacks were also served automatically, so she didn't have to see anyone. In a certain sense, the place was perfect.

But she couldn't stay here forever. She stroked the cut on her stomach and clenched her jaw.

Natsumi had no idea what Shido and Kotori were up to, but it wasn't hard to imagine that it would be bad news for her. They were obviously planning to get revenge one way or another. Maybe they intended to eat her after fattening her up. In which case, she could understand why they would give her such delicious food.

"Well, that's not gonna happen!" she declared to the empty room.

The gash Ellen had inflicted on her was healing nicely. If everything went well, she'd be recovered enough to manifest Haniel in a few more days. When she could do that, the walls of this room would be the same as paper. Literally. She could escape whenever she wanted to then.

There was also the option of getting Lost and fleeing to the parallel world. But on top of the physical toll shifting between worlds took on her, there was also the possibility that she would be yanked right back into this world the instant she returned to the parallel world, so that was an option she'd rather not choose if she could help it. Although the probability of this was very low, if she ran into that Wizard Ellen again when she was pulled back over to this side, she might very well be killed.

At any rate, at the moment, building her strength and healing had to be her top priority. With this in mind, Natsumi shoved the remaining bits of breakfast into her mouth.

She had barely finished the last bite when the door flew open and a group of people marched into the room to surround her.

"Huh…?!" Natsumi let out a cry of bewilderment. She hurriedly looked around and realized that these were all familiar faces.

Shido and Kotori. And Tohka and Yoshino, whom Natsumi had selected as suspects in her little guessing game.

Kotori went without saying, but Tohka, blessed physically and yet not boastful, and Yoshino, drawing the attention of boys with her timid demeanor, were also the types of girls Natsumi hated. But that wasn't the issue at the moment. The more important problem facing her was that the group surrounding her was equipped with a burlap sack and rope.

"Wh-what...on earth?!" Natsumi shouted in confusion, and Kotori snapped a finger out at her.

"Get her!" Kotori shouted.

""""Roger!"""" Shido, Tohka, and Yoshino jumped into action as one. A burlap sack came down over Natsumi's head from behind, and her field of vision went dark. Kotori's subsequent order led to the rope being wound tightly around her body over top of the bag.

"Nnn! Nnnnnnn?!" Natsumi panicked and struggled, but it was no use. Her hands and feet were tied securely with the rope, and she couldn't move. All she could do was squirm and wriggle like a seal rolling along the waves in the ocean.

And then someone lifted up her body and shouldered it.

"So now what do we do, Kotori?" Tohka's voice came to her through the rough burlap.

"Right. Bring her this way." Kotori said.

"Mm. Got it!" Tohka started to move, carrying Natsumi.

Where are you taking me?! The worst possible scenarios played out in Natsumi's mind. Dumped out of the sack onto a chopping board?! Or maybe they would toss her *and* the sack into a pot of boiling water?!

"I—! I—! I'll make you so sick if you eat meeeee!" she howled.

But Tohka didn't pay her the slightest mind.

Natsumi felt a steady rocking back and forth, informing her that they were moving toward their destination.

She had no idea how much time passed after that. Around the time she grew tired of shouting and started to go limp against Tohka's back, Tohka abruptly stopped and slowly set her burden down. The rope was then untied and the sack removed. A gentle light dazzled Natsumi's dark-accustomed eyes.

"Ungh..." Shielding her face with a hand, she waited for her eyes to adjust, and then her jaw dropped at the unexpected scene spreading out before her. "Wh-what is this place...?"

There was no enormous cutting board, no giant pot burbling like it sat over the flames of hell.

In the room, which was illuminated with a warm light, there was a bed just big enough for one person to lie down on, and Natsumi could smell something like flowers in the air. It was an almost disappointingly gentle space.

While she stared in obvious bafflement, a girl in something like a nurse's uniform stood to one side of the bed and waved her hand.

"Helloooo! Welcome to the one-day limited pop-up spa, Salon de Miku!" the girl said, and smiled at her.

Natsumi knew this face, too. She was pretty sure the girl's name was Miku Izayoi. With her ample and ostentatious boobs hanging down garishly, she was the type of girl Natsumi hated.

"H-hey, what *is* this...?" Natsumi said slowly.

"What?" Shido replied. "Miku told you just now. It's a spa. We're going to give your skin a treatment."

"...?!" Natsumi grew even more confused. "Hold on. I don't get it. Why—?" Her shoulders jumped up. She had realized the true objective of Shido and his friends. "Ha... Ha-ha! So that's it, huh? You're gonna make me do this and then get your kicks laughing at the uggo who fell for your stupid lies? Oh! Ha-ha... You all have seriously weird hobbies. You're as rotten as I—"

"Hup!" In the middle of Natsumi's speech, Kotori gave her a karate chop on the crown of her head.

"Ow!" She automatically clutched her head and shrank back. "Wh-what're you doing?!"

"It's not even your looks we have to do something about." Kotori sighed. "It's this negativity and persecution complex. Listen, you're fine. Just lie down. We've got a full day ahead, and you're slowing things down."

"No!" Natsumi snarled. "Why are you forcing me when I know you'll just laugh at me?!"

"Okay, you—," Kotori started, and Shido set a hand on her shoulder to stop her.

"So then, Natsumi, how about this?" he said. "We'll 'transform' you today in whatever ways we can think up. If we pull it off, that's our win, and you have to listen to us for real. But if you think nothing about you's changed by the time we're done, then we lose, and you can do whatever you want."

"Whatever I want meaning what?" she asked slowly.

"Right." Shido thought about it for a second. "All I can think of is letting you go wherever you feel like. How about it?"

"...!" Natsumi's eyes grew wide.

Perhaps Kotori hadn't expected Shido to make this proposal; she jabbed him with her elbow. "Whoa, Shido."

"It's fine, though," he said. "We've got no other card to play. So, Natsumi? I don't think it's such a bad deal."

"..." Natsumi narrowed her eyes as if examining Shido's true motives.

Either way, once she recovered, she could use Haniel to escape. But given that Shido had Spirits like Tohka and Yoshino on his side, she couldn't reject the possibility of them getting in her way. And to start with, this contest was no contest at all. No matter how hard they worked, she highly doubted they'd be able to do anything with this scraggly wreck of a person. It would be irritating to go along with them and get laughed at, but if that meant that she'd be able to make a clean getaway in the end, she did feel like it wasn't such a bad deal.

"Fine," she said finally. "In that case, I'll do it."

"Yeah?" Shido said. "Okay then, do what Miku tells you to."

"..." Natsumi turned a silent glare on him, but he returned her gaze without so much as flinching.

"We'll teach you, Natsumi," he told her.

"...Huh?" She frowned. "What?"

"That girls don't need an Angel to transform themselves." He grinned at her.

"...!" Her ire unreasonably roused by this, Natsumi whipped her face away from Shido.

"Okay, she's all yours, Miku." Shido waved and went out a door on the opposite side of the room.

"Yes, yeees. Please leave everything to meeeee!" Miku spun around and looked Natsumi up and down. "Aaaaall right, should we get started, then? First things first. Let's get those clothes ooooff you."

Miku stepped toward Natsumi, waggling her fingers in the air. For some reason, Natsumi felt like her eyes had a different sparkle to them than when Shido had been there.

"Huh? Uh!" Natsumi automatically took a step back. She would rather have died than let this woman with teats like a Holstein cow see her skinny body. And above all else, she instinctively detected some kind of danger to her person.

But Kotori, on standby behind her, grabbed her shoulders and kept her locked in place.

"Hey!" she cried.

"You just don't know when to give up, do you?" Kotori chided her. "Be a good girl."

"It'll be fiiiine. I promise I'll be gentle." Breathing heavily, Miku peeled Natsumi's hospital gown off.

"Eeep! Eeep!" Natsumi kicked and struggled, but her resistance was futile. Soon enough, she had not a stitch on her and was being made to lie facedown on the bed. "Wh-what are you going to do to me?!"

"Hee-hee-hee! You diiiid give us quite the fright, after all. I'm going to return the favor teeeen times over," Miku said, grinning. She reached out for a bottle on the shelf and began to pour the dubious liquid inside on Natsumi's back.

"Eeeaaaah!" she shrieked. "What?! What is it?!"

"Come, come! No fighting now. It's a super luxurious essential oiiiil." Miku caressed Natsumi's skin gently, tracing her fingers lightly across the other girl's back.

"Ah! Fwaaah!" Natsumi heard a strange cry coming from her own mouth at the sensation, which she'd never experienced before.

"Hee-hee-hee!" Miku giggled. "Feels niiiice, doesn't it? I wouldn't say I'm quite as good as a professional, but I am preeeeeetty good. Honestly. You really need to take proper care of your skin."

"I—I mean," Natsumi protested, "it doesn't matter..."

"First of all, I knooooow you say you have no confidence in yourself," Miku said. "But I just can't accept that when you're not making any effort at all. While there aaaaare natural-born beauties in this world like Tohka, the women you're so jealous of are all working hard to be beauuuuuutiful."

"It's just... Someone like me, whatever I do...," Natsumi said, and felt a haze fall over her mind. Maybe because she hadn't really been getting enough rest and the fatigue had been building up in her, or maybe because Miku's massage was too relaxing, she was overcome with a sudden sleepiness.

"I...am..."

Natsumi fell fast asleep.

"Okay! We're all doooone!"

"...!" Natsumi woke with a start at Miku's voice.

At some point, her body had apparently been turned over, and she was now lying faceup. Although a towel had been laid across her chest, she still felt awkward somehow.

"How was it?" Miku asked.

"Ummm." Natsumi lightly stroked her own skin, and her eyes widened in surprise. "H-how...?"

She couldn't immediately believe it. Her rough, dry skin had been transformed into something smooth and moist like a baby's.

"Hee-hee-hee!" Miku laughed merrily. "People are always surpriii-ised after their first spa experience. Of course, your skin won't stay like this indefinitely, but it is impressive, isn't it?"

"Wow." Natsumi stared down at herself. "Huh? Is this...really *my* hand?"

"Yes, it is withoooout a doubt actually yooours. Hee-hee-hee! When I get a reaction this good, it makes me excited about the next room."

"What?" Natsumi looked up at Miku.

"Now, once you're dressed, you're coming this way."

Kotori, who had apparently been waiting on a chair in a corner of the room, stood up to lead the way. Next to her, Tohka and Yoshino were asleep, leaning up against each other.

Natsumi slipped on the hospital gown she had shed earlier, went through the door at one end of the room, and advanced to the next room.

"Keh-keh-keh! You are well met. This is the domain of the Yamais!"

"Praise. I shall commend you on your nerve alone."

Twins with the same face greeted her, adopting some kind of heroic pose. The peerless battle formation of the slender Kaguya and the glamorous Yuzuru. They were indeed the kind of women Natsumi hated.

"Wh-where...?" Natsumi opened her eyes wide and looked around. There was a tall mirror on the wall and a large chair set up facing it. She knew this place at a glance. It was...a hair salon.

"Guidance. Please come this way," Yuzuru said, and took Natsumi by the hand.

"Ah!" Natsumi was sat down in the chair so a cloak could be tied around her neck to cover her body. And then the chair back was lowered so that she was staring up at the ceiling. "Wh-what are you...?"

"Continuation. You'll understand soon enough." Yuzuru turned on the tap by her hand and sprayed comfortably warm water on Natsumi's head before lathering up some shampoo and beginning to neatly wash Natsumi's long hair.

"Ungh. Ah..." Natsumi squirmed a little at the unfamiliar sensation of someone else washing her hair.

"Keh-kah-kah-kah!" Kaguya let out a high-pitched laugh from where she stood next to the chair. "Yuzuru's shampooing technique brings the ultimate bliss! After all, those are the hands that snatched victory within a single minute in our ninety-first contest, a shampooing war!"

"Smile. You were quite ticklish, Kaguya," Yuzuru said quietly, as she rinsed the lather away and began to massage Natsumi's scalp with a conditioner that smelled quite nice. It all felt so good that Natsumi very nearly fell asleep once more.

"Alternate. All right. Now it's time for Kaguya's specialty," Yuzuru said, bringing the chair back up once she had finished conditioning and toweling Natsumi's hair dry.

Kaguya pulled out a pair of barber scissors from the belt on her waist and spun them deftly around a finger. "Keh-keh-keh! Entrust yourself to me!"

"Y-you're...cutting my hair?" Natsumi gasped.

"Indeed! But there is no need to fear! My skills become obvious when you examine the results of the hair-cutting battle that was our ninety-second contest!"

"You two really do battle about anything, huh?" Kotori said with a wry smile from where she stood off to the side watching.

"Aye!" Kaguya threw her head back smugly and came to stand behind Natsumi. "I have no intention of clipping too aggressively. However, the pained ends of the hair are a heavy burden! I shall not let you alone escape! Scatter like petals through my blade technique, Kaiser Schere Wind!"

She made the scissors in her hand clack as she flew around the ends of Natsumi's hair.

A half an hour or so later, Natsumi's hair, full of split ends, had been cleaned up to a surprising extent.

"No way." Natsumi stared at herself in the mirror. "Wow."

"Heh... Well, you see the results." Kaguya blew on the tips of her scissors like a gunman at the end of a duel before slipping a finger through the handle, spinning them around, and tucking them away on her hip again. Next, she pulled out a hair dryer and a comb, then began to intently blow-dry Natsumi's stiff hair.

"Keh-keh. This hair has quite the will of its own, but that is not to say all hope is lost. Strike them down while wet, and these hairs shall rise up no more."

"U-uh-huh…" Natsumi nodded, a bead of sweat rolling down her cheek.

But Kaguya appeared to be as skilled as she bragged she was. Natsumi's constant bedhead became impossibly light and breezy. It even seemed to shine a little somehow.

"Keh-keh! Well done. You may proceed to the next area."

"Assent. Come this way."

"Umm…"

The next area. Natsumi furrowed her brow anxiously at these words.

But she couldn't stop now that she'd come this far. She opened the door at the far end of the room. Trailing along behind her were Kotori and the Yamai sisters, Miku, and Tohka and Yoshino, who had apparently awakened while Natsumi was getting her hair cut.

On the other side of the door was the largest of all the spaces she'd been in thus far. Every bit of the large floor space, which was illuminated by fluorescent lighting, was taken up with neatly folded shirts, coats on hangers, skirts, and more.

Yes. The space closely resembled a so-called boutique.

"Wh-what…?" Natsumi whirled her head around to examine the area and met the eyes of Kotori behind her.

"Heh-heh!" Kotori grinned. "Spa, hair salon—next up's gotta be picking out some clothes, right?"

Tohka bobbed her head up and down.

"H-huh?" Natsumi said. "Hang on. I'm not really—"

"Yeah, yeah." Kotori clapped her hands, cutting Natsumi off. "You can say your piece later. Okay, gang."

"Mm!"

The other girls closed in on Natsumi, carefully curated outfits in hand, before she could even process what was going on.

Tohka pressed a cute dress up against Natsumi as she spoke in a bright voice. "Something like this'd be good, right? So cute!"

"Mm-hmm. It's maybe not bad. But could be a bit cold for the season," Kotori said, stroking her chin.

Yoshino held up a coat while Yuzuru pointed to a hat.

"So then with this..."

"Suggestion. I would recommend this, as well."

"Mm. Nice. Woh-kay. Give this a try for now, Natsumi." Kotori pushed the other girl toward a changing room as if it was the most natural thing in the world.

"Hey! You can't just go and decide for me!" Natsumi shouted.

"Yes. Indeed," Kaguya agreed. "It is as Natsumi says. Restraint would be best. We shall select the article most appropriate for her." She offered up an outfit in black with plenty of chains and belts.

"Aah! No, that won't do at all. I'm telling you, thiiiis suits little Natsumi so much better," Miku objected, and held out a different outfit. This one had plenty of ruffles, a dress fit for a doll.

"..."

Without a word, Natsumi accepted the items from Tohka, Yoshino, and Yuzuru, marched over to the dressing room, and yanked the curtain shut.

"Wh-why?! Why would she reject our obsidian outfit?!" Kaguya wailed on the other side of the curtain.

"Aaaah! I was so sure this would be cuuuute!" Miku moaned.

"Dammit! What is this? What even is...?" Natsumi grumbled, as she put a hand to the ties of her hospital gown. She was absolutely not feeling it, but if she complained about the items she had taken into the dressing room with her, she might get stuck with Kaguya's or Miku's even worse choices. Glumly, she took off her hospital gown and changed into the dress and jacket before popping the hat on her head.

"Mm. You still not done, Natsumi?" Tohka asked.

"If she still won't play nice, you and me'll strip her, Tohka," Kotori said.

Natsumi sighed heavily, braced herself, and finally pulled the curtain open, looking totally different from when she had closed it.

The eyes of Tohka, Kotori, Yoshino, the Yamais, and Miku all focused on her.

"Ungh." She squeezed her eyes shut and clenched her teeth to try and suppress the urge to vomit welling up from deep in her throat. Eventually, their sneering laughter…

"Mm! This works."

"Hmm. Personally, I feel like something a little more chic would suit her better. I don't know."

"Oh… How…about this?"

"Yes. Let's go with something a little booolder. What about thiiiis?" …did not come.

"Huh?" Natsumi opened her eyes at the unexpected voices she was hearing. There before her were six girls and one puppet with smiling or serious faces. "Um." The unexpected reaction confused her.

Kotori held out an expensive blouse and a monotone skirt. "Here, Natsumi. Try this one next. I think it'll work better on you."

"Uh. Um," she stammered.

"Go on. Hurry up." Kotori grabbed her shoulders and pushed her back toward the dressing room.

And for the next three hours, Natsumi was dressed up in outfit after outfit after outfit.

And it wasn't just clothing. She was also decorated with shoes, hats, and all kinds of accessories, watches, and glasses (just for show, of course), and in the later stages of the expedition, she was even persuaded to strike some poses. She felt like a dress-up doll or an avatar in an online game. She didn't know what was what anymore. By the time they found an outfit that everyone agreed on, Natsumi was thoroughly exhausted.

"All right! This is definitely it."

"Yes… It's wonderful."

"Mm-hmm, mm-hmm. This might be iiiiit."

"Mm! I think it's good!" Tohka laughed brightly and bobbed her head up and down.

Kotori turned her eyes on Natsumi. "Okay then. Next up, the last room, finally."

Everyone jumped, and Natsumi felt sweat springing up on her forehead at this unusual reaction.

"Wh-what…?" she asked anxiously, and the Yamai sisters giggled merrily.

"Keh-keh! Go, and all will become clear. Now then, this way."

"Assent. The most powerful assassin is waiting there for you."

"A-assassin?!" Natsumi gulped loudly at the ominous word. To be quite honest, she didn't really want to proceed.

But Miku gave her a push and half forced her to open the door to the next room. "Come ooooon, let's go."

"Oh. Uh…"

This place, designated as the last room, was the smallest of any of the spaces so far. A chair sat alone in the middle of the room, and next to it stood a girl with her back turned to the door.

Natsumi had never seen this back before. So was this the "most powerful assassin" the Yamai sisters were talking about?

She swallowed nervously, and the girl slowly turned around.

She was tall with a somehow androgynous face, and hair that curled like smoke down her back and was adorned with a four-leaf clover–shaped barrette.

But for some reason, Natsumi got the impression that she was somehow desperate or maybe despondent—like she was really pushing herself to hold it together. When Natsumi looked closely, she saw tears in the corners of the girl's eyes.

"You made it!" the girl declared. "This is the final room in the Natsumi transformation project!"

"Wh-what are you going to do?" Natsumi asked.

"Okay, just gotta get through this," the girl muttered, before forcing up the corners of her mouth and crossing her hands above her chest.

Natsumi could see lip gloss and eyeliner, concealer, and a variety of other tubes and jars wedged between the girl's fingers.

"Th-that's—!"

"Yes. I shall transform you with my makeup skills!" She snapped a tube of lip gloss out at Natsumi. The force of it caused Natsumi to unconsciously take a step back.

And then Natsumi shook her head vigorously. "Wh-what are you talking about? There's no way I'm going to change with just—"

"You *will* change!" the girl insisted.

"Could you not just say stuff at random?! I mean, someone like me...!"

"Do you really believe that? That people can't change with just some makeup?"

"O-of course I do!" Natsumi said, and the girl tucked away the makeup items wedged between her fingers into a pouch around her waist. Then she slowly brought a hand to her own neck.

"Then—" The girl ripped off what appeared to be a small bandage on her neck. "Then what about the fact that I'm actually a boy?!"

"Huh?!" Natsumi's shoulders jumped up at the boy's voice that was suddenly coming from the girl's mouth. "What? How is this...?"

She was perplexed for a moment, but then she quickly realized something. She had heard this voice before.

"N-no way." She gasped. "You're Shido?!"

"Yes! I am!" The girl (?) nodded forcefully.

When she really looked, Natsumi could see traces of Shido Itsuka in that face. The moment she realized this, she unconsciously cried out, "P-pervert?!"

"..."

"Oh! He's hurt. That hit him where he lives."

"Well, he can't exaaactly deny it."

She could hear the voices of Kotori and Miku from behind her. It seemed they were all in on it.

"A-anyway!" Spirit slightly broken, Shido pulled himself back together and turned his eyes on Natsumi once again. "In a surprise twist, my makeup techniques have reached such a level that I can make you think a boy is a girl! Now that I am in this place, I can give you self-confidence!"

"No, uh, I mean, you might have gotten better, but you also have the person's natural look in there, too, to a certain extent."

"That's so truuuue. I did think he was a giiiirl at first, after all."

Kotori and Miku began to whisper once again. Shido's gaze sharpened.

"C-could the outfield be quiet?" he snapped. "At any rate, this is the contest, Natsumi! With all my heart, body, and technique! I will transform you!"

"...!" Natsumi's face stiffened, but she gritted her teeth. "Fine. Then why don't you do that? But don't forget. If I don't think I'm transformed, then you lose!"

"Mm-hmm. I know. Now, if you don't mind!" Shido bowed and gestured her toward the chair. His manner was almost like that of a servant waiting upon a princess.

Natsumi obeyed and sat down. Immediately, she was looking at Shido's face extremely close-up. Even though his own features remained, he really was done up like a cute girl. The only word for it was *impressive.*

What if I could...?

"N-no, no..."

She shook her head as if to chase away the thought that started to flit through it. No matter how amazing Shido's powers of makeup were, it was impossible, unachievable. In which case, there was no point in getting her hopes up. A half-hearted hope would only deepen her inevitable disappointment.

As if guessing at Natsumi's thoughts, Shido stretched his lips into a smile. "It'll be okay."

"…!" Natsumi blushed and hung her head. "Um. One thing?"

"Sure. What is it?" he asked. "Go ahead and say it."

"It's pretty creepy when you speak in a boy's voice with that face."

"…"

Shido looked a little sad somehow and put back on the bandage he had peeled off earlier.

"O-okay, here we go!" he said, his voice slightly higher pitch now, sounding like he was trying to get back into the rhythm of things. "First, the basic of all basics, we wash your face. Skip out on this step, and your makeup's not going to sit right!"

Following Shido's instructions, Natsumi very thoroughly washed her face, took a bit of toner in her hands, and patted it into her entire face.

"Perfect. Now leave the rest to me," Shido said, and got to work on a base, using a powder puff to apply a light layer of foundation. "I'll tell you right now, Natsumi. I'm not trying to use makeup to change your face into someone else's. I'm just highlighting your features. I'm merely helping you break free of this thinking you're fixated on, that you're worthless."

"H-hmph. You're a master talker, if nothing else," Natsumi said grumpily, but Shido simply smiled quietly.

And then he dabbed her cheeks with blush, did her eyes, and finally painted her lips with a gloss.

"Okay. All done." He exhaled, tucked his tubes and applicators away in his pouch, and stood up.

"Th-this is finished?" she asked. "You went pretty light on me, huh?"

"I told you. There's no point in it if I completely hide your actual face. But this is more than enough. See?" He pointed behind the chair.

"Wh-what…?" She looked back and saw Tohka and the others jammed together, waiting. She caught sight of something like a plank with fabric draped over it in their midst.

She quickly caught on. It was a mirror. They were going to show Natsumi herself.

Here, she finally noticed the expressions on the faces of the girls gathered around the mirror. They all had their eyes open wide in surprise.

"Wh-what? What is it?" Natsumi asked, unsettled.

Tohka nodded dramatically as she grabbed one corner of the fabric draped over the mirror. "Mm! You should take a look!" She yanked the cloth covering off to expose the large mirror.

"Huh?" Natsumi looked at the girl reflected in the glass, and for a second, she was at a loss for words.

Her bird's nest of a hairstyle had been neatly pulled together, leaving traces of her natural waves, and it shone under the lights. Her unhealthily pale skin had a soft sheen she'd never seen on herself before, and clad in an adorable outfit, she looked like a graceful young lady.

But what surprised her above all else was her face.

With more of it exposed now after her fringe had been neatened up, this face was definitely Natsumi's. If she had to list the changes to it, they would be the faintest hint of pink in her cheeks; her eyes, which had a slightly sharper outline; and her lips, which had been painted a pale rose color—she could only see these very trivial differences.

But each and every one of those small differences made her face dramatically cuter. The change was so striking that, for a second, she wondered if she wasn't looking at a mirror but rather a screen with some video feed projected onto it.

"Th-this is...me?" Natsumi murmured, as she patted her cheeks and stared at herself in disbelief.

"Yup." Shido put a hand on her shoulder. "No mistake. It's you, Natsumi."

The girls crowded around began to speak up all at once.

"Mm! So pretty!"

"Hmm. This works, doesn't it? So? What do you think?"

"Well, weeeell. Say, Natsumi? How would you like to come oooover to my house?"

Natsumi felt like one of them had a slightly different light in her eyes than the others, but rooted to the spot in surprise as she was, she didn't pay it too much mind.

"So, Natsumi? Who's the winner of this contest?" Shido asked, looking into her eyes through the mirror.

"...!" Natsumi gasped. For just an instant, she had thought the girl in the mirror was...cute. "Ah... Ah..."

Her eyes darted around the room, and her legs shook.

She should have been happy. Delighted. A few hours ago, she would never have believed the appearance she had so desperately loathed could be transformed to this extent. But it was so far beyond anything she had expected in such a short time that her brain couldn't completely process it.

What? What is going on right now? Who is this? M-me? And, like, what is with these people? Why would they do all this for me? After I did such terrible things to them. Have they lost their minds? And the contest? What contest? They said I lose if I'm cute. But that means I definitely lost, it's not even a question. I mean, this is super cute. Huh? But. Wait. Huh?

"H-hey, Natsumi?" Shido asked hesitantly.

"Ungh. Ah. Ah. Aaaaaaaaaaaaaaah!!" Natsumi didn't understand anything. She ripped at her hair and shrieked as she ran back the way she'd come.

Eventually, Natsumi slipped on the floor of Salon de Miku, fell rather spectacularly, hit her head, and passed out. She'd clearly been tremendously upset. The hair they'd worked to clean up was all over the place, and the seams of her clothes had been pulled apart.

They put the unconscious Natsumi back into her hospital gown and laid her down once more in the isolation space. Perhaps she was having some kind of bad dream—from time to time, she groaned where she lay on the bed.

"Hmm." Kotori put a hand to her chin as she stared at the monitor outside the room.

Seeing the troubled look on her face, Shido scratched his cheek. "I guess it really was too much for her. I never dreamed she'd hate it that much, though."

"…No, I don't think it's that," Reine said from where she stood next to Kotori.

"Huh?" He cocked his head, and Reine showed him a screen in her hand. It displayed Natsumi's face and several different numbers.

"…Mental status, mood, likability—they've all pulled up from the worst levels. Of course, they're still far from a level where you'd be able to seal her power."

"Th-they all went up?" Shido asked.

"…Mm-hmm." Reine nodded. "It seems that she definitely did not hate her makeover. Well, I suppose she still must have been extremely confused and disoriented."

"Ohhh…" Shido nodded in understanding. He did actually feel like the way Natsumi had panicked was out of the ordinary.

"…Most likely, she's not used to being complimented outside her transformed state. She's convinced that she's worthless, that no one would bother with her if she didn't transform. Despite the fact that somewhere deep down, she wants someone to properly see and accept her, she simply has no confidence."

Reine held up a finger and continued.

"…As a result of my examination and analysis, I've learned that the number of times Natsumi has quietly manifested in this world is far beyond any of the other Spirits. She seems to be a powerfully curious Spirit. She's also well versed in this world's customs. I can't particularly recommend this way of going about things, but since Haniel can also falsify paper, she likely hasn't had any issues with making purchases."

"Makes sense." Shido nodded. "But then why would she have so little confidence in herself?"

"…No, I think that might be exactly why," Reine mused, troubled.

Shido recalled something Natsumi had said. "Now that you mention it, she complained that in this world, when she was just Natsumi, no one wanted to have anything to do with her."

"...A string of negative experiences probably warped her worldview. Because she *can* change her appearance freely and without a thought, she must've gradually come to reject her original self," Reine hypothesized. "The key here is not her actual physical appearance, but whether or not she can believe anyone will see and accept her."

"That's a tough one, hmm?" Kotori sighed and shrugged. "But, well, if she actually does *want* to be seen as herself, that gives us a way in. We basically just have to build up her confidence. Then she'll start being able to accept what we say to her. Her attitude'd soften a bit, too, I bet."

"It would be great if we could actually do that," Shido said.

"We won't get anywhere by being pessimistic," Kotori told him. "At any rate, we'll give it a go. First thing tomorrow, we start Natsumi's rehabilitation."

"Rehabilitation?" he asked. "What are we going to do, exactly?"

"Well..." Kotori paused like she letting her mind run free. "If we just need to convince her she's cute, then maybe it'd be good to have someone outside all this tell her what they think straight up."

"But no matter how many times we tell her she's cute—"

"That's why we need an outsider." Kotori cut off Shido's protest. "It won't work with you and the Spirits since you were part of her makeover. Even if *we* think we're being honest in our assessment of her, there's no point in us saying anything if *she* thinks we're looking at her through rose-colored glasses. I could get some people together through Ratatoskr, but if possible, someone completely unconnected with us would be preferable. Anyone spring to mind, Shido?"

"Huh? Hmm, let's see." Shido stared off into space for a moment, and the face of a friend popped into his mind. "Oh!"

"Aaah, you're really gonna set me up with a girl? A friend in need really is a friend indeed!"

The following day, Tonomachi slapped Shido's back happily, seemingly having completely forgotten the chaos at school.

Yes. The person Shido had called to act as Natsumi's rehabilitator was his classmate Hiroto Tonomachi. Of all of Shido's friends, he was the most excitable and amenable, and he also loved to talk. Plus, because he was also a victim of Natsumi's guessing game, he wasn't entirely unknown to her. The thinking was that this would somewhat ease the tension of a first meeting.

"I'm not actually setting you up, though," Shido told his friend. "And, like, she's kind of shy, y'know? So could you maybe just chat with her a bit?"

"You got it," Tonomachi assented, pounding a fist against his chest. "You leave everything to me, best pal. I'll make sure to invite you to the wedding."

"Ha-ha..." Shido felt Tonomachi was already flying off into dreamland before he'd even met Natsumi. Maybe he picked the wrong person for this job.

"Anyhoo, Shido, what is this place? I mean, you blindfolded me and shoved me into a taxi. To be honest, I'm kinda nervous about where I even am, okay?"

Shido and Tonomachi were sitting in what appeared to be the lounge of a chic hotel. Naturally, Ratatoskr couldn't exactly unleash Natsumi on the outside world, so they'd modified one corner of the underground facility. Guests and staff could be seen here and there, but they were all Ratatoskr personnel.

"I-I'm telling you, don't worry about it," Shido said, sweat springing up on his brow. "I'll make sure you get home okay, too."

"I'm sure there's no way, but, Shido, I gotta check." Tonomachi's gaze sharpened abruptly. "This girl."

"Huh?"

Tonomachi was looking at him like he could see right through him, and Shido unconsciously jumped in his seat.

Tonomachi couldn't have known about the Spirits. But did he actually suspect something was up? Shido didn't want to say anything to prejudice Tonomachi before he introduced him to Natsumi. He frantically racked his brain for something innocuous to say.

However.

"Is she maybe some superrich-princess type?!" Tonomachi asked excitedly.

"What?" Shido gaped in reply.

"The sheltered daughter of a rich family, sickly, constantly stuck at home." Tonomachi continued rapturously. "Her sole delight in this world is seeing the photos her friend—Itsuka—shows her of school. And then one day, she spots a boy in those photos. 'Aah, I wish I could meet such a fine man!' So she musters up all her courage and asks the friend to bring the man to her! Like that kind of thing?!"

"Uh. Yeah. Well… Basically." Shido went along with his friend's fantasy.

"Mmmmm!" Tonomachi squirmed in his seat, completely lost in his dream. "My glory days have arrived! Thanks, Shido! Even after I marry into wealth, you and me'll still be buds!" He grabbed Shido's hand and pumped it up and down.

"Uh. Uh-huh…" Shido's conscience pained him somehow.

But Tonomachi appeared not to notice Shido's inner turmoil. He whirled his head around. "So? Where is my sweet darling at?"

"Uh, over there." Shido pointed at a chair farther back.

Sitting there in a cute outfit and beautifully made up, with an *extremely* grumpy look on her face, was Natsumi.

"…" Natsumi sat down in the chair, indignant.

When she woke up that morning, Kotori had come barging in and dragged her here without a word of explanation.

What exactly was this place? Because she was unaccustomed to being around people when she hadn't used Haniel to transform herself, she was quite uncomfortable. Every time one of the guests around her laughed, she worried that her name was the butt of every joke.

And then.

"Hey! Hello there!"

She heard an overly excited voice in front of her and jumped in her seat.

She looked up to find a boy standing before her. With a face she'd seen before. Yes, this was Shido's classmate. She was pretty sure his name was...

"H-Hiroto Tonomachi... Why are you here?" Natsumi said suspiciously, trying not to meet his eyes.

Tonomachi's eyes widened in surprise. "Y-you know my name?! And Tohka and Kaguya can still never remember it!" he said, voice choked with emotion.

Creeped out slightly, Natsumi pulled her chair back a bit.

But Tonomachi appeared not to notice this and plopped himself down in the opposite seat, practically vibrating with excitement. "Nice to meet you! What's your name?!"

"...N-Natsumi..."

"Natsumi! What a great name!" Tonomachi said overly familiarly, and Natsumi eyed him suspiciously.

"...!"

First, this guy appears out of nowhere, and now he's saying what? Did Shido or Kotori ask him to come and say nice things to me or something?

That was it. That had to be it. It was completely unthinkable that he would randomly compliment Natsumi otherwise.

"Aah, I didn't think you'd be so cute. I really gotta thank Shido!" Even while Natsumi was considering all this, Tonomachi kept speaking, sounding entirely thrilled.

Natsumi sniffed indignantly. "How much?"

"Huh?" Tonomachi stopped and stared at her.

"How much are they paying you? It's gotta be a pretty hefty chunk of change."

"What are you talking about?" Tonomachi craned his neck in confusion, and she couldn't see any sign on his face telling her she'd hit the mark.

"..."

Natsumi frowned. What was this? Normally, when you called a person out, they would react a little at least. And given how skilled she was at observation, there was no way that Natsumi wouldn't notice the slightest twitch or stiffness.

Which meant... It couldn't be. Did this guy really think Natsumi was cute?

"...!"

Natsumi felt her heart suddenly start racing. *No. No way.* It had to be an act. But the Natsumi in this moment was different from the Natsumi of the day before. This was the Natsumi made over by Shido and his friends. What if...?

She darted her eyes around the room, looking everywhere but at Tonomachi.

Meanwhile, he pressed a hand to his forehead. "Aah, this is a real shock, okay? You're so cute. I'm practically dizzy over here!"

"...!" Natsumi gasped, and her face stiffened up at Tonomachi's words.

Practically dizzy. → Dizzy... Meaning: Head spinning, on the verge of passing out. → When I look at you, my head spins, and I nearly pass out. → Just looking at you is disgusting, you pig.

"I. Knew. Iiiiiiiiiiiiiiiit!" Natsumi yelled, and flipped the table over.

"Wh-whoa?! Wh-what's wrong, Natsumi?!"

"What's wrong? What's *wrong*?! You're sneering at me! You think I'm a dolt! It's not like I wanted to be like this, you know!"

When she began to race around the lounge screaming, the staff hurried over to pin her down.

"P-please calm down, miss!"

"W-withdraw! Bring her!"

"R-roger!"

"What are you doing?! Let go of meeeeeeee!"

Natsumi was unceremoniously dragged away.

"So that didn't work."

"That did not work."

Shido and Kotori sighed in unison after having somehow managed to calm Natsumi down again.

Tonomachi, on the other hand, had already been delivered to the surface. After Natsumi abruptly lashed out, he had seemed completely and utterly shaken. But then he said, "*So she really does have a serious illness... But I'm gonna be there for her!*" And Shido couldn't decide whether that was rude or heroic.

"She's even more negative than we thought," Kotori said finally. "Looks like we went too far springing an outsider on her with no explanation."

"So then what do we do?" Shido asked.

"We've already considered our next step. Kannazuki." Kotori snapped her fingers.

"Sir!" A tall man appeared from who knew where exactly. This was Kotori's second-in-command, vice commander of *Fraxinus*, Kyouhei Kannazuki.

Shido looked at this man, whom he had met any number of times before, and furrowed his brow unconsciously. But that was only natural. He was the very picture of a dodgy producer in brown sunglasses and a cardigan with the sleeves tied around his neck and draped over his shoulders instead of properly on his arms.

"Kannazuki?" Shido said. "Why are you dressed like that?"

"Heh-heh. I'm our ace in the hole. I shall teach that negative little kitten her own charms." Kannazuki gave him a confident thumbs-up.

"What is it now?"

About three hours after the Tonomachi thing, once she was breathing evenly again, Natsumi was left alone this time in a place that looked like a café.

She'd been told that they were going to take her to somewhere else after this, so could she please wait here a bit? But where exactly were they going to take her? She wondered, hanging her head a little to avoid the gazes of the people around her.

And then.

"Oh? Oooooh!"

A tall man, looking very suspect in sunglasses and a cardigan tied over his shoulders, approached her and leaned in to peer at her face.

"Wh-what...?!" Natsumi said, alarm bleeding onto her face, and the man slapped his forehead theatrically.

"Whoopsy! Excuse me! I work in the industry. This is me," the man said, as he pulled a business card from his pocket and held it out to her.

She timidly accepted it and dropped her gaze to it. She read the card aloud. "Ratatoskr Productions Chief Manager, Kyouhei Kannazuki."

"Yes! We represent models and other talent, along with producing films and TV programs and the like!" This Kannazuki or whoever he was bowed in an exaggerated way and continued excitedly. "Apologies for the sudden intrusion, miss! But have you ever considered modeling?!"

"Huh?" Natsumi's eyes flew open. "M-modeling... You mean in magazines and stuff?"

"Yes! That kind of modeling!" Kannazuki nodded with excitement.

But Natsumi sighed in response.

This model thing. Natsumi recalled the magazines and TV shows she'd seen in this world. If her memory was correct, a model was a slender, tall, and attractive woman. The Natsumi after her Haniel transformation was one thing, but it was obvious that this was not the sort of job Natsumi could do in her current form. This man had to be one of those scummy guys. He was definitely some crook who tricked girls with honeyed words and extorted huge sums of money from them under the pretext of singing lessons or something.

"Sorry, but I really hate jokes. A model's someone taller and more stylish, not someone like me," Natsumi said self-deprecatingly.

"Oh, I would never joke about such things!" Kannazuki shook his head. "Stylish? Ha! What meaning is there in what is nothing more than a large chest?! None! Rhetorical question! True beauty is the exclusive domain of immature flowers about to bud in preparation for spring! Magnificent! The way you are now is truly marvelous! You are the one with the beautiful body! Stay this way forever!"

"…!"

Kannazuki pressed closer to her, breathing heavily, and she unconsciously pulled back. Just like Tonomachi before him, he didn't look to her like he was lying.

He was a little creepy, but maybe he really did think she was "a flower about to bud." Were there also people in this world who were interested in girls like Natsumi? But it was over the top to say that the Natsumi now had a beautiful body…

"Ah!" Her eyes flew open.

Natsumi has a beautiful body. → *Natsumi has a nice physique.* → *Her appearance is unfortunate, but it seems like there are no issues in terms of performance.* → *Your organs would likely fetch a high price.*

"Mu—! Murderer?!" Natsumi half shrieked, and leaped up from her chair.

"Oh-ho!" Kannazuki stepped back in surprise. "What is the matter?"

"S-stay away from me! You can't fool me! I'm onto you!"

"I would never fool you! Now, this location is a bit crowded, don't you think?" Kannazuki said, as he grabbed Natsumi's arm. "If it's all right with you, my office is—"

"Eeeeaaah!" Natsumi shrieked and slapped Kannazuki's cheek before dashing away.

"Another no go."

"That was indeed another failure."

Shido and Kotori sighed in unison once more as they watched the scene play out.

"Aah, ha-ha! This is embarrassing." Kannazuki laughed, looking distinctly unembarrassed. There was a mark like a maple leaf on his cheek, and one of his sunglass lenses was cracked.

"Well, you were definitely way too creepy," Kotori remarked. "But Natsumi's pessimism is more deep-rooted than I'd imagined. We're gonna have to take it down a notch."

"Take it down a notch?" Shido raised a dubious eyebrow. "Meaning?"

"Right." Kotori nodded to herself. "Rather than complimenting her first thing, we'll start with getting her to understand that if people have a regular conversation with her, that doesn't mean they're laughing at her."

"Mm-hmm. And how specifically?"

"Have her order from a fast-food restaurant or something."

"We're really lowering the bar here," Shido said with a pained smile. But judging from her reactions so far, that level of interaction was probably best for Natsumi. They had a better chance starting low and slowly pushing up from there.

"Woh-kay. Then we'll move on to the next set." Kotori flicked the stick of her Chupa Chups up. "I'll bring Natsumi out of her room, so you get everything ready."

"So what exactly is it this time?"

Natsumi glared in annoyance at Kotori and Shido sitting across from her.

She had been brought to what appeared to be a hamburger joint. The restaurant was bustling with students still in their school uniforms and parents with children, all chatting busily.

"Nothing special," Kotori said naturally. "I'm just kind of hungry."

"Uh-huh. Right," Shido followed up awkwardly. "Just hungry."

Natsumi looked at them with suspicion in her eyes.

"So. Sorry, but could you go order?" Kotori asked. "I'll give you the money. You choose what we get."

"H-huh?!" Natsumi cried. "Why should I—?"

"It's fine. Here." Kotori pressed some bills into Natsumi's hand. "Don't lose it."

"H-hey!" Against her will, Natsumi was pushed toward the counter. "Ngh!"

There were so many things she didn't like about this, but she was stuck. She trudged over to one of the registers and came to a stop, head hanging.

"Welcome! Are you ready to order?" a girl with long bangs on the other side of the counter said with a smile.

Natsumi tried to keep her heart from pounding its way out of her chest as she replied in a trembling voice, "Th-three...ham...burgers..."

"Sure thing! That's three hamburgers, right?"

"Y-yes..."

"Did you want fries with those?" the cashier asked, still smiling.

"...!" Natsumi's eyes flew open.

Did you want fries with those? → In this case, "fries" → "fried pota-toes." → The combination of carbohydrates and oil is very fattening. → Your scrawny body would be a bit better if you put on some weight, you know?

"God. Damn. Iiiiiiiiiiiiit!"

"What?!"

Natsumi launched a corkscrew punch at the register, and the cashier jumped.

"You don't have to tell me that, okaaaaay?! I mean, it's not like I *chose* this bodyyyyyyyyy!"

"Uh... M-miss?!"

"N-Natsumi!"

"Shido! Hold her down!"

She heard Shido's and Kotori's voices from behind. Natsumi was quickly restrained and returned to her original room.

Chapter 9
I'd Like to Believe

"*Humpty-Dumpty has completed docking.*"

"*All systems go. No issue with orbital maneuver.*"

"*Arriving at target location in approximately five hours.*"

"*DSS-009, airship* Heptameron, *has reached its designated position.*"

The reports came one after the other from the speaker set up in the conference room of DEM Industries' UK head office. Murdock followed the various data streams displayed on the LED screen before his eyes and nodded exaggeratedly.

"Where is MD Westcott now?" he asked.

"*He hasn't moved from his hotel. We believe that if a spacequake alarm was ordered, he would evacuate to the shelter in the hotel or to the nearest DEM-related facility.*"

"Durability?"

"*If the* Humpty-Dumpty's *impact margin of error is within ten kilometers, there will be no issue.*"

"And what about *Second Egg*?"

"*Deployed. We are ready for further orders.*"

"Excellent."

"*Second Egg*?" Simpson turned dubious eyes toward Murdock.

Murdock returned his gaze, the corners of his mouth curling up.

"For insurance purposes. It's nothing you need to concern yourself with."

"…" Simpson stared at Murdock silently for a moment, then finally turned his eyes back to the LED. He looked dissatisfied and also disturbed by Murdock.

It's a good omen. Murdock twisted his lips up with satisfaction and let his eyes wander over the various faces there in the conference room.

"We are proceeding exactly as planned," he announced. "We will no doubt receive notice of MD Westcott's passing this evening. The company funeral will likely be quite the affair. I would recommend that you consider now what condolences you will offer."

The executives glanced at one another before allowing awkward smiles to cross their faces.

Despite the fact that today was the day they executed their plan, it seemed that they were still afraid of making an enemy of MD Westcott. Most likely, some among them were maneuvering to push all the blame onto Murdock if, in the worst case, the mission ended in failure.

Murdock snorted, too quietly for anyone else to hear. He was fine with that. It was a small price to pay if it meant these cowards would show their agreement with this mission with that one bit of meager insurance. If this mission did fail, Murdock would be done for regardless as the ringleader. So it was the same either way.

Normally, he wouldn't have wanted to run the risk of an information leak and plan a mission with the entire anti-Westcott faction. However, the fact was it would have been impossible for Murdock to carry out this scheme on his own authority, considering the personnel and airships required for mission execution and the concealment of all related information. No, actually. It wasn't impossible. But at DEM Industries, there was only one person who could carry out a mission of this scale at will—Westcott.

That didn't mean, however, that there were no advantages to bringing this collection of idiots along for the ride. Simply put, the men here now would know only too well the reason for and cause of Westcott's disappearance.

When news of Westcott's death arrived, an emergency board meeting would be held and a new ultimate authority decided on. And when that conversation began, who exactly would come first to the minds of the men here? There was no question the assassination of the previous MD would be a terrible scandal. If anyone got a hold of the information, they would have had to have been eliminated. But the executives in the room now were coconspirators. On top of that, they were, to a person, cowards. If Murdock named himself the next MD, not one of them would raise a voice in protest.

To that end, Murdock was fully committed to playing the role of a man desperate and crazed enough to put a mission like this into action. So that when Westcott disappeared, the fear of him they held in their hearts would be transferred to Murdock.

"Actually, perhaps that's not quite it," Murdock murmured, as he opened and closed his now bandage-free right hand.

He was indeed playing the crazed man, at most as a means to seize hearts and minds. But from the moment his arm had been sliced off by Ellen Mathers, he had the feeling that slowly but surely, he really *was* losing his mind.

Murdock grinned and began to hum a nursery rhyme to himself as he watched the video of *Humpty-Dumpty* on the LED screen.

"Humpty-Dumpty sat on a wall, Humpty-Dumpty had a great fall... ♪"

Curled up cross-legged on the bed, blanket draped over her head, Natsumi muttered to herself, "What... What... What...?!"

She felt like a flow of incomprehensible information was filling her head and spilling from her mouth as words. Thoughts spinning and racing, Natsumi had been groaning in this position for a while now, unable to process this confusion with no outlet.

"What exactly...is *with* them...?!" She yanked at her own hair as the figures of those boys and girls danced through the back of her mind.

Why would they pay so much attention to her? Why would they do all this for her?

She could've understood it if she was the Natsumi turned into a beautiful young woman using Haniel's powers. Transformed Natsumi was gorgeous enough to make anyone stop dead in their tracks and turn heads. Men hiding their love and lust deep inside, and women their envy and jealousy, offered up all kinds of flowery words to that Natsumi.

But these people were different. They were saying that *this* Natsumi—the way she was now, not transformed with Haniel's power—was cute.

This word was supposed to have been something Natsumi had desperately longed and waited for. But…because it was the first time she'd ever been told she was cute, she was simply unable to take it in.

"It's… It's obviously a lie. Ha. Ha… R-right. They're all taking me for a ride. I mean…," she muttered, as she lifted up the blanket covering her head. Now she could see her own reflection in the mirror on the wall.

The made-over her. The cute her.

"…!" She gasped and yanked the blanket back down. Her thoughts grew even more chaotic.

After all, Natsumi was supposedly ugly. She was a hopeless disaster, grotesque, not cute at all. She had to be. She was obviously ugly.

"Huh…?" A question popped into her head.

I'm obviously ugly?

Why? How was it obvious? In what way?

"A-anyway…I can't believe that they would do that stuff to me, their enemy, without a reason. They must… They have to have some kind of objective." Natsumi placed a hand to her chest and quietly said, "Haniel."

Her hand shone faintly, and something like a mirror appeared in her palm.

"Ngh." The cut on her stomach hurt, but it wasn't so bad that she couldn't stand it.

She turned the mirror downward, toward the bed, and changed it into a bed with a hole big enough to hide one person. Then she pulled together all the stuffed animals under the blanket and used Haniel to turn the pile into a perfect copy of a sleeping Natsumi.

She wriggled around inside the blankets and slipped into the hole in the bed, leaving the dummy Natsumi on top of it. And then she made Haniel shine for a third time to close the surface of the bed up behind her and transform it, the floor, and the walls so that she could slip through them, like she was digging a tunnel.

"Perfect." A few minutes later, Natsumi came out into a deserted hallway, restored the wall to its original shape, and looked around.

There were several security cameras in the room where she'd been locked up, but this would fool them for the time being. That said, however, if she didn't touch her meal when it was served, there was the risk of someone coming in to check on her. She didn't have that much time.

In order to quickly finish up her mission here, Natsumi called to mind the faces of the people she'd met. The most convenient was probably...

"...Th-that one." Natsumi nodded and turned Haniel's mirror on herself.

The mirror flashed, and her body shone faintly. And then her silhouette gradually warped until a few seconds later, Natsumi had become an entirely different person.

A girl small in stature wearing a red military uniform. Long hair tied up in two black ribbons, determined expression on her face.

Yes. Shido Itsuka's little sister, Kotori Itsuka.

Natsumi guessed that she was the most appropriate choice for walking around this facility and observing people.

But there was that one thing. She wore her hair in pigtails. The star of the cute-hairstyle world, pigtails. A hairstyle you couldn't even attempt unless you had supreme self-confidence. Natsumi loathed this hairstyle. So much that she had even considered turning herself into someone with national authority, revising the laws, and making pigtails illegal. But she would have to suck it up for now. It went against every bone in her body to disguise herself as a sly pigtailed girl, but efficiency was the priority at the moment.

"Whoops! I forgot." Natsumi yanked off a button in an unremarkable spot of her jacket and held it up to Haniel.

The trail of fabric she'd pulled off with the button emitted a pale light, then transformed into a small lollipop with a stick. She was pretty sure this was what Kotori was always sucking on.

"Mm. I guess that's about it," she said in a voice that sounded quite different from seconds earlier, and snapped her fingers. Instantly, Haniel turned into particles of light in her hand and melted into the air.

"Now then..." With Haniel gone and herself completely transformed into Kotori Itsuka, Natsumi took a couple deep breaths before starting to walk slowly down the hallway.

So she wouldn't be seen as suspicious should she run into someone, she searched her surroundings with eye movements alone. She caught sight of doors with electronic locks from time to time in the wide, long hallway. She didn't yet know the entire layout of this building, but she could easily tell that it was a fairly large facility.

"Seriously. What *is* this place?" Natsumi muttered under her breath. The only thing that was certain was that this was a facility to which Shido, Kotori, Tohka, and the others had some kind of connection, but she didn't know anything beyond that. To start with, boys and girls their age shouldn't have been able to make free use of a place like this. Maybe they belonged to some kind of organization, which would mean they had some serious backing.

When she thought about this, a chill naturally ran up Natsumi's spine. They couldn't actually be planning to capture the Spirit Natsumi and use her as a lab rat or something, right? Thoughts like this flickering through her mind, she examined the hallways, which were so reminiscent of a hospital or some kind of research facility.

"Hmm? Commander?" a voice called out to her abruptly from behind.

"...!" Jumping imperceptibly, Natsumi looked back to see a woman with long bangs and the same uniform as Kotori in a different color.

Seeing Natsumi, the woman tilted her head to one side curiously.

Natsumi looked closely and realized this was the cashier at the hamburger shop that Shido and Kotori had taken her to the day before.

"What are you doing here?" the woman asked. "Is something the matter? Didn't you say before that you were returning to *Fraxinus*?"

"Oh, I thought I'd check in on Natsumi before I left." Natsumi spoke in as steady a voice as she could manage.

"Oh, you did?" The woman nodded, seeming entirely unsuspicious. "Well, she is a difficult one. If this keeps up, we'll never seal her."

"Seal? What are you talking about?" Natsumi cocked her head to one side, and the woman's eyes grew wider.

"Well, her Spirit power, of course. Have Shido kiss her and lock away her Spirit power. Isn't that what our organization is for?"

"…!" Natsumi's eyebrows jumped up, but she acted cool so as not to let the other woman see how upset she was. "Ohhh. That's right. Sorry. Maybe I'm a little tired."

"Ha-ha-ha! It's no wonder. Well, I'll return once my duties here are finished, so I'll see you then," the woman said, and bowed slightly.

Natsumi let out a sigh of relief in her heart as she replied, "You will. Oh! Right. Can I ask you one thing?"

"Hmm? What is it?" the woman asked.

"You know where Tohka and the others are?" Natsumi said evenly. "I wanted to talk to them a sec."

"Tohka?" The woman thought for a moment. "Let's see. I feel like she was in the break area over there."

"Yeah? Thanks. Okay, see you later."

"Oh! Yes. Good-bye." The woman walked away without a look back.

Natsumi watched her go and then turned in the direction she had indicated and started walking once more. Quickly but not so quickly as to draw attention.

She had both gained and lost in her interaction with that woman. The gain was the information on Tohka's location and the fact that Kotori was not currently in the facility. So Natsumi was guaranteed not to encounter the girl she'd copied no matter how much she strolled around the place. And bigger than anything else was the fact that she had found out the objective of Shido and his gang. It all came together for her now. She'd wondered what their true motives were, but she never dreamed they were trying to lock away her powers.

"I *thought* this was weird. Those dirty cheats!"

But at the same time, it was now known that there was someone in Kotori's form in the facility. When that woman finished work and returned to this *Fraxinus* or wherever, there was a chance that the real Kotori would have questions for her. Natsumi couldn't be too leisurely about this.

After walking for a bit, she caught sight of a small space up ahead. There were vending machines, a smattering of chairs, Tohka, and Yoshino.

Natsumi grinned as she walked over to them. "Hey, Tohka. Yoshino."

"Mm?"

"Oh… Hello."

"Ohhh? Why, if it isn't little Kotori!"

Tohka, Yoshino, and Yoshinon on Yoshino's left hand turned in that order and greeted her.

Natsumi smiled and waved before coming to a stop in front of the bench they were sitting on.

"Hey, Kotori! This place is amazing! They let you drink juice for free!" Tohka cried with great delight.

"Did you…want a drink, too, Kotori?" Yoshino asked.

"What's your poison? I can snap out and hit that button for you," Yoshinon said, and jabbed left and right, shadowboxing.

With a pained smile, Natsumi shook her head and crossed her arms as she opened her mouth and asked what she most wanted to know in that moment. "I'm good for now. Anyway, what do you all think about this Natsumi kid?"

Yes. She was sure that these girls were laughing at Natsumi deep down inside. Maybe they just had to put her in a good mood in order to seal her powers, but in this place where Natsumi was not, they were certain to spill their true, malicious feelings.

"What…do we think?" Tohka cocked her head to one side.

What an annoying girl. Or maybe she just didn't want to be the first one to bad-mouth Natsumi. In which case...

Natsumi sniffed and lowered her eyes as she continued speaking, almost spitting out the words. "Don't you think that Natsumi jerk is disgusting? We fawn over her the teensiest bit, and she gets all carried away. Even though she's an uggo. It's so pathetic, I can hardly stand it."

I got the ball rolling. Now, spill it.

Natsumi raised her eyes a little to peek at Tohka and Yoshino. She was sure that now that they had an excuse, now that they weren't the ones who'd started talking smack, ugly expressions would take over their faces.

However.

"Mm?"

"Huh...?"

"Hmm?"

All she saw were two people and one puppet looking at one another, completely baffled.

"Huh?" Natsumi's eyes widened at the completely unexpected reaction.

"Kotori." Tohka furrowed her brow. "What's the matter with you? It's not like you to talk like that."

"Uh. Um... I don't. Think Natsumi is. Creepy...at all," Yoshino said.

"That's right. What's up, Kotori? You in 'tired from commander duties' mode?" The puppet appeared to raise its eyebrows in concern.

"Wha...?!" Natsumi unconsciously took a step back. "Wh-what's going on with all of *you*? You don't have to pretend you're so saintly. I mean, you're all thinking it, right? Like, what a hassle it is to have to put that sad sack of a girl into a good mood."

"What are you saying?" Tohka said, her face brightening. "That's not true, you know? I had so much fun picking out clothes!"

Yoshino and Yoshinon both dropped their heads forward as if in agreement.

"Yes... Natsumi was. So pretty..."

"Aah, Shido's makeup was incredible, huh? Maybe I'll get him to

do mine one of these days." Yoshinon twisted in a little dance of glee, and Tohka and Yoshino burst into cheerful laughter at the silly movement.

"B-but... That's... It's not..." Natsumi let her eyes roam, flustered, and began to tremble.

These girls really mean what they're saying.

This fact was shocking enough to put cracks in Natsumi's identity.

Several possibilities were provided in an instant by her brain. Maybe they had seen through her disguise and knew that she had turned into Kotori, meaning this was a prearranged performance. Or maybe someone they loved had been taken hostage and they were being forced to say nice things about Natsumi. *No, no, wait. Maybe—*

These absurd ideas appeared and disappeared again. But none of them had any persuasive power in the face of the smiles Tohka and Yoshino were wearing.

"N-no way. How...?" Forgetting that she was pretending to be Kotori, Natsumi felt her fingertips trembling and then saw three girls approaching from up ahead. The Yamai sisters and Miku.

"Keh-keh! And for what reason do you throng here?"

"Petition. Please allow Yuzuru, Kaguya, and Miku to join as well."

"Hee-hee! It's a teeeea party!"

"K-Kaguya, Yuzuru, Miku!" Natsumi cried, as if entreating the new visitors.

Perhaps surprised at this, the three girls stopped in their tracks, their eyes wide as saucers.

"Hmph. What is the matter, Kotori? Your countenance is nothing of the ordinary. Did you perhaps open the gate to hell sealed in darkness?" Kaguya said these curious words, while she struck a pose.

Natsumi ignored this and continued speaking as she tried to regain her composure. "L-listen to this, gang. There's something weird with these kids here."

"Question. Weird how?" Yuzuru asked curiously.

Natsumi kept going, a dry smile crossing her lips. "They're saying this stuff about Natsumi being pretty, that it's no hassle to hang out with her, okay? Ha-ha-ha! Makes you laugh, huh? I mean, just looking at that uggo brings you right down into gloom town."

The three girls frowned dubiously.

"Hmph. It is not your way to speak such strangeness, Kotori. What has happened? It is rather early to be crazed by the moon's poison."

"Puzzlement. These are words that I cannot believe are Kotori's."

"You can't taaaaalk like that about Natsumi. You're going toooo far, and now I'm angry!" Miku put a hand on her hip and puffed out her cheeks indignantly.

Natsumi felt her heart start to beat faster. "H-hang on a minute. She's an evil Spirit who tried to lock us up inside a mirror and become us! Think about this rationally! Why are you taking the side of someone like that?! Have you lost the program here?!" she shouted at the top of her lungs, having now completely forgotten that she had transformed into Kotori.

Even while the girls were all baffled by Natsumi's actions, they glanced at one another and pondered this.

"Well… It's true that Natsumi did give us a real scaaaare," Miku said, seemingly in agreement, finger pressed against her chin.

"Right?! So then—"

However.

"But…if you're going to say thaaat, I did plenty of less than nice things myself." Miku continued. "I don't think I'm ready to say that it's all water under the bridge, but at the very least, I waaaant to be friends with Natsumi."

Everyone else began to nod.

"Yeah! Same here!"

"M-me…too. I'm. Sure we can…be friends."

"From what I hear, she chose Yoshinon as the one to turn into, right? Aah, that's a girl who knows quality."

"Hmph. Well, this is the very villain who pressed us into such a situation. There is value in having her in our ranks."

"Assent. She has a bright future."

"…!" Natsumi staggered backward, at a loss for words.

Everything was all over the place in her head. She gritted her teeth and left the break area without looking at anyone's face.

"Umm. I guess the living area is B Section." Shido walked at a leisurely pace down the hallway of the Ratatoskr underground facility where Natsumi was being kept.

The facility was a fair distance from the Itsuka house, and because he'd taken the long way to make sure that Ellen and anyone else from DEM couldn't follow him, it had been a bit of work just to get here.

That said, however, as long as Natsumi was in this place, Shido couldn't exactly not show his face. He'd brought some clothes and his toothbrush from home so that he could borrow a room here and stay for a while.

He was just turning a corner in the hallway when he felt a *bump* against his chest.

"Whoops!" He lowered his gaze and saw familiar hair tied up in two bundles. "Hey, Kotori."

"..."

For some reason, Kotori merely glanced at his face wordlessly.

"What?" he asked. "You seem sad. What's wrong?"

"Nothing. Nothing's wrong," Kotori said in an obviously glum voice.

He scratched his head, and Kotori turned her face away and moved to walk off, as if to say she didn't want him to bother her anymore.

"Oh!" he called out to stop her. "Hang on."

She stopped where she was but didn't look back at him. "What? I'm actually busy, you know."

"Oh yeah. Sorry. I'll be quick. It's about Natsumi."

"...!"

The moment he uttered Natsumi's name, he saw Kotori's ears perk up.

"What about Natsumi?" she said, turning to look at him sharply.

He knew that she was quite sensitive when it came to Natsumi, but he felt like this was a bit extreme.

"Y-yeah. It's about Natsumi's meals," he said, feeling overwhelmed, but he could tell that Kotori's mouth had relaxed.

"Heh-heh." She chuckled. "Aah, so your true nature is finally revealed."

He frowned. "Huh?"

"Forget it." She waved a dismissive hand. "So what do you want us to do? Maybe we shouldn't give her anything to eat for the next few days? Or you want to try mixing poison into her food?"

"Uh." He scowled, sweat beading on his forehead. "What are you even talking about? If this is a joke, I'm not laughing."

Kotori furrowed her brow dubiously. "So then what? What do you want us to do?"

"So for supper today, could you maybe let Natsumi out of that room?" he asked.

Kotori looked up at him. "What for?"

"Well, everyone's here," Shido explained. "So I was thinking it might be good if we could all eat together."

"Huh?" Kotori's jaw dropped for a moment before she twisted her lips up in a sneer. "Ohhh, I get it. You mean to seal her power. You're a piece of work, too, huh? Luring Natsumi out like that and stealing her Spirit power from her."

Shido frowned at this very un-Kotori-like statement. "What are you talking about? The objective of Ratatoskr is to seal the Spirit powers and allow the Spirit to live safely and happily."

"Huh?"

"And this isn't just for likability, okay? I mean, I know she's in isolation, but it's still sad to eat by yourself. And I bet everyone wants to talk with Natsumi as well."

"…"

"Maybe Natsumi will soften up a bit, too, eating some delicious food… Uh, Kotori?" Shido's eyes grew wide.

The reason was simple. Huge tears had begun to spill out of Kotori's eyes. Her cheeks and eyes were bright red, her shoulders were shaking, and she hiccuped every so often.

A shiver ran up Shido's spine at this abnormal behavior from his normally tough little sister. "H-hey, what's wrong?! Did I do something?!"

"Noth..." She sniffled. "Nothing...!"

"No, but it's not nothing! Don't worry! I'll make enough for you, too—"

"Shut up! Go to hell! You jeeeeerk!" she shouted, and ran off down the hallway, wiping her tears away with her sleeve.

"Hey! Kotori?!" He couldn't exactly just leave her like this, no matter what she said. Shido hurriedly chased after her.

But when he turned the corner, his feet stopped.

"Huh?" He knew that Kotori had just turned this corner, but she had apparently vanished like mist. "That Kotori, where did she...?"

He looked all around, but she was nowhere to be found. A lone Chupa Chups with the wrapping not yet taken off was on the floor as if to signal that Kotori had been there.

"She even dropped her lollipop. Something must've happened." He picked the candy up to give back to her when he saw her later, and then left with no other choice, he went back the way he had come.

After he'd walked for some time, his phone began to vibrate in his pocket. The name displayed on the screen was Kotori Itsuka. He hurried to press the ANSWER button.

"Hello? Kotori? Are you okay?"

"*Uh? Why wouldn't I be okay?*" Kotori replied, like she had no idea what he was talking about.

"No, it's just, a second ago, you—"

"*Whatever,*" she said, cutting Shido off. "*We've got a situation. We just got a message from the supervisor there. Natsumi's escaped from her room.*"

"Wha...?!" Shido gasped. "Escaped?! But how? I thought she still wasn't able to use her Angel?!"

"*Maybe our estimates were too generous,*" Kotori replied. "*Was she able to use her transformation powers even in her unhealed state? Maybe that was it. She left a dummy of what we assume are transformed stuffed animals and has completely disappeared. Most likely, she tried to turn into someone else and flee. You got any ideas?"*

"Ideas... I mean, I don't..." His eyes flew open. "Oh!"

◇

Approximately two hours later, Shido was back above ground.

Although all personnel had been mobilized to search every nook and cranny of the underground facility, they hadn't seen any sign of Natsumi anywhere. Shido, Tohka, and the others had learned from Shiizaki's testimony that Natsumi had likely transformed into Kotori, but given that it wasn't guaranteed that Natsumi would stay in that form forever, this wasn't much of a clue to go on.

"Natsumi," he murmured to himself, as he trudged down the residential street. Given that Natsumi was no longer there, there was no point in him being underground, so he'd shouldered his bag with his extra changes of clothes and was walking back to his own house.

In the end, Shido hadn't seen Natsumi smile even once after she was taken into custody. All she'd done was hate everything he, Tohka, and the others did. She'd steadfastly refused to open up to them.

But Shido couldn't believe that was how Natsumi truly felt. He just couldn't.

A dog, long-abused by people, actually wanted to frolic and play, wanted to be cuddled and spoiled, and yet reflexively feared human beings.

Which was why none of his team would say a bad word about Natsumi. There was no one bullying her here. He'd believed that their feelings would reach her at some point if they just persisted in trying to communicate them to her.

"Wait." He stopped and shook his head slightly.

Maybe this was nothing more than his own selfish conviction. A tiny pang of regret shot through his heart.

Natsumi might have gotten strong enough to be able to use her transformation powers, but that didn't mean her wound had healed completely. She wouldn't come away unscathed if the AST or DEM Wizards found her in her injured state.

If the reason for Natsumi's flight lay with Shido and his friends… Thinking about this, his thoughts inescapably went to a very dark place.

"That wouldn't happen." His face stiffened slightly, and he began walking again as if to pull himself free of that train of thought.

Soon enough, his house came into view. As he stepped through the gate, he dug around in his pocket to pull the key out and then pushed it into the keyhole.

"Hmm?"

He stopped, confused. He turned the key, but there was no response. Thinking this suspicious, he pulled on the doorknob, and the door opened without any resistance whatsoever.

He was certain he had locked the door when he left the house. And he couldn't think of anyone who would've come home before him.

"Weird. I thought everyone was still under—" Shido had gotten that far when his eyes flew open in surprise. "Natsumi?!"

Yes. Natsumi would have known the location of the Itsuka house. He threw the front door open, kicked his shoes off, and raced toward the living room.

And stopped.

Just as he'd expected, there was a girl in there.

However.

"Wha…?" Surprise colored his face, and he was stuck for words.

"Excuse me for intruding." The young woman sitting on the sofa in the living room was definitely not the one Shido had been expecting.

Nordic blond, like the sun was always shining on her, blue eyes. There, in his living room, was the DEM Industries Wizard, Ellen Mathers.

"Ellen?!" he yelped. "What are you doing here?!"

"I will explain in detail. Please sit," Ellen said, gesturing toward the sofa opposite her.

"What…?" Shido acted like he was hesitating and poked at the phone in his pocket. This was an emergency. He had to tell Kotori right away.

"…" Ellen raised her right hand, and before he knew it, his phone was floating up and sliding through the air into that hand.

"Wha…?!" He gaped at her.

"It would not be a particular issue for me were you to call for help, but having our discussion interrupted would be annoying. I do apologize, but I'd appreciate you allowing me to hold on to this for the time being." Ellen placed the phone she'd taken from Shido on the table and turned her gaze on him. "I will say this for form's sake. The entirety of this house is my Territory. I do not recommend resisting me."

"Ngh." Shido gritted his teeth in frustration before sighing and settling down on the sofa across from Ellen.

"So what exactly does DEM want that they would go so far as to barge into someone's humble home?" he said sarcastically, offering up a bare minimum of resistance.

But Ellen didn't look the slightest bit perturbed by this as she stared hard at him. "There is no issue. I merely came to ask you a simple question."

"A question?" He eyed her suspiciously.

"Yes. I will be direct. Where is the Spirit Witch you carried away the other day?" Ellen asked in a quiet voice.

Shido clenched his hands into fists. "Come on already! There's no way I'd tell you that!"

The truth was, Shido would've liked to ask her the same question. But he kept that to himself. He wanted to avoid letting her know that Natsumi had escaped. Making her think that Natsumi was still under the protection of Ratatoskr would no doubt keep Natsumi safe.

But Ellen's calm facade did not waver in the face of Shido's wild cry. She continued calmly. "Well, I suppose you wouldn't. And I didn't think you would tell me so easily as that."

"Yeah?" he replied. "Then could I ask you to leave? I have to make supper."

"You cook it yourself?"

"Is that a problem?"

"No. I think it's wonderful."

"...Well, thanks," Shido said, without bothering to try and hide his hostility.

Ellen let out a short sigh as she stood up. She slowly walked across the living room and let her gaze roam as if examining the state of the room and the kitchen before opening her mouth.

"It's a bit small, but it's quite a well-kept home. I can almost picture the happy family gathering every evening."

"..." Shido frowned, unable to understand what Ellen was getting at. He highly doubted she was being sincere.

But Ellen appeared not to be interested in his response. She spoke again in her lovely voice. "Who exactly would be in this happy family scene, I wonder? You. Kotori Itsuka, Tohka Yatogami, Yoshino, and perhaps the Yamai sisters and Miku Izayoi would be around the table. They would no doubt all eat your meals with some relish. A happy space like something out of a picture. Please, I would ask that you cherish this."

"What are you trying to say?" Shido asked, frustrated, and Ellen turned her entire body toward him. Perhaps because the window was behind her, he couldn't catch her expression in that moment, backlit as she was.

"Who do you think this happy family owes its existence to?"

"What?" Shido furrowed his brow at the unexpected question. "Well, Kotori and Ratatoskr—"

"That is incorrect." Ellen rejected Shido's response without hearing it to its end. "This wonderful home exists thanks to Ike and myself. We overlook your existence, we do not deign to kill you, and so you are able to enjoy a moment of peace."

"Wha...?" Shido felt a trickle of sweat run down his back.

Ellen didn't sound the least bit like she was joking or messing around with him. She was serious. She did not doubt for a millisecond this absurd and violent theory.

"...!"

Ellen was a Wizard; in other words, although she had machinery embedded in her brain, she was still human. And yet for some reason, Shido felt a greater sense of strangeness—no, foreignness in her than he did when talking with the Spirits.

"I'll be brief." Ellen slowly raised a hand and turned it toward him. This was all she did, but for some reason, Shido abruptly felt like he was having trouble breathing. Maybe she had lowered the oxygen level in the area through manipulation of her Territory. Or maybe she was pressing that Territory up against Shido's mouth and nose. Or she might have been overwhelming Shido with simple pressure.

"Shido Itsuka, and along with you, Princess, Efreet, Hermit, Berserk, and Diva. In return for the continued safety of the aforementioned, please give me the location of Witch."

"Y-you can't be—," he stammered.

"Please make no mistake," she cut him off without a thought. "This is the greatest concession you will receive. You do not have the option of choice."

"Ngh…"

"It's simple arithmetic. For one Witch, the security of the other Spirits will be guaranteed for the time being. I believe this is quite a good deal," Ellen said, as if it was the most natural choice in the world.

But Shido took a deep breath and snorted his disdain. "Sorry, I've always been bad at math."

"Is that so? How unfortunate."

Shido's words were no doubt in the realm of what she had expected. Ellen slid a hand inside her jacket without showing the slightest disappointment and pulled out something that looked like a knife handle without the blade.

For a moment, Shido didn't understand what it was, but he watched as Ellen narrowed her eyes, and a blade of glowing light appeared at the end of the handle. He swallowed hard.

"Now then. We will spend some time together until you are able to properly calculate profits and losses. I look forward to seeing exactly how many lashes you can endure." Ellen smiled for the first time as she turned the blade of light on Shido.

◇

"No signal at point A!"

"Nothing at point B!"

"The faint Spirit signal from the isolation area also drops out along the way!"

On the bridge of the airship *Fraxinus*, floating fifteen thousand meters above Tengu, the voices of the crew flew back and forth.

Kotori had mobilized all the measurement devices on *Fraxinus* to chase after the Spirit signal of the missing Natsumi.

However, the results were as noted.

"Tch!" Kotori clicked her tongue softly where she sat in the captain's chair, hand on her chin. "I expected this, but still. We really can't get a Spirit signal, then."

Given that they couldn't pick up a signal, the search was mainly proceeding through the autonomous cameras they had crawling the city. But those wouldn't be much use against Natsumi when she had the ability to transform. There was no way she'd be out there in a form that Kotori would easily recognize when she knew she was a fugitive. If she'd turned into some random passerby, then finding her would be nearly impossible.

"This is bad, hmm? It'd be great if she'd come around to harass Shido again, but if she's on guard against us and doesn't show herself, then… it'll be impossible to seal Natsumi's Spirit power," Kotori said, troubled, and issued orders to the crew working on the lower deck.

"It's inefficient to search without any leads whatsoever. Focus on the places where Natsumi has appeared at least once. The abandoned theme park where Shido and Natsumi first met, my house, Shido's school, and the mountain where we took Natsumi into custody."

""""Yes, sir!"""" the crew replied, and the video displayed on the monitors began to shift locations.

"Hmm?" Minowa said, facing her personal display.

"What is it?" Kotori demanded immediately. "Natsumi's signal?!"

"N-no, it's not that…"

"What? Spit it out. Exactly what are you seeing?"

"Could you please look at this?" Minowa tapped at her console, and the screen she was seeing was displayed on the bridge's main monitor.

The observation area had been enlarged to the maximum possible to search for Natsumi's signal, and at the end of the sky, a single, suspicious signal could be seen.

"What's that?" Kotori asked.

"Judging from the altitude and orbit, it appears to be an artificial satellite or something of that nature," Kawagoe said, looking at the screen.

Kotori frowned and turned her gaze on Nakatsugawa. "Can you get me video?"

"Yes, sir! Just one moment!" Nakatsugawa tapped at his console, and a point, a mere speck, was displayed on the screen. The video was of poor resolution after being zoomed in on several times over.

"It does appear to be…an artificial satellite. But why on earth would it be…?" Mikimoto furrowed his brow and stared at the screen intently. "It's very faint, but there is a magical signal! And it's…explosive magic!"

"What did you say?" Kotori frowned. Explosive magic. Put simply, this meant a Realizer-powered magical bomb. "What is going on? Why would something like that—?"

She brought a hand to her mouth in sudden realization.

"No… They wouldn't do something so stupid."

"C-Commander? What's the matter?" Nakatsugawa asked, adjusting his glasses.

"If…" Kotori swallowed hard. "And this is just a hypothetical. If a satellite was to drop onto Tengu, what do you think would happen?"

"…!!"

The entire crew was rendered speechless.

" "
…

The taste of salt spread through Shido's mouth. The sweat running down his cheeks had slid across his lips and reached his tongue.

With Ellen's laser blade thrust at him, he frantically racked his brain for some way out of this situation.

But Ellen gave him zero openings. If he made like he was going to run, she would skewer his legs on that blade of light in a heartbeat.

As if guessing at Shido's thoughts, Ellen sniffed lightly. "It's pointless. There is only one way you leave this place alive. You disclose the location of Witch."

He feigned a sigh. "Sorry, but I've been amazingly forgetful lately."

"In that case, allow me to assist your recollection," Ellen said, and slowly walked toward him.

"Ngh." He tried to at least step back for a little breathing room, but his body wouldn't comply. It seemed that Ellen had bound him with her Territory.

"There's no artistry in suddenly taking a finger. I know." Ellen licked her lips and brought her laser edge up to the side of Shido's head. Almost as if—yes, like she was about to cut his ear off. "I will ask you one last time. Do you really have no intention of telling me Witch's location?"

She looked at him with cold eyes, and Shido felt his heart pounding painfully in his chest.

This woman would do it. She would lop off his ear without even hesitating. He was forced to remember the pain of when she had once pierced him with her blade, and his legs started to shake.

However, Shido brought the corners of his lips up in a smile and somehow managed to keep his voice from shaking as he spoke. "My ear was actually itchy just now."

"Is that so?" Ellen said, narrowed her eyes abruptly, and tightened her grip of the hilt of her laser blade.

But then.

"…!"

Shido's phone sitting on the table made a chirping sound and eased the tension suffocating the room.

Ellen's attention was also taken up by the inane ringing. For a split second, he was able to move his body, which had been bound by her

Territory. He'd heard from Kotori that no matter how much of a master a person was, it took a tremendous amount of focus to maintain a Territory without a wiring suit.

"Fwah!" If he missed this opportunity, he'd never get another chance. Shido yanked his arms up and shoved Ellen as hard as he could.

"Ngh!" A look of anguish came across her face as she tumbled backward.

Sending up a prayer of thanks to whoever had called him with such impeccable timing, he ran.

But just as he was about to leave the living room, his body froze in place once again.

"Wha…?"

"That was quite something." Ellen slowly pulled herself to her feet, a quiet anger tinging her voice.

Three seconds hadn't even passed. And yet during that fleeting moment, Ellen had redeployed her Territory. Her powers of concentration were fearsome.

"Although it was mere chance, I will have you pay for setting me on the ground," she told him.

"Ngh."

"Additionally, you touched my chest. You will die now."

"It was an act of God, though!" Shido shrieked, but Ellen paid this no mind. She brought her laser edge to his face once more.

But now Ellen's phone started to vibrate.

After arching an eyebrow, she answered it, still maintaining her Territory.

"Yes, this is me. Is there something the matter?" Ellen said without taking her eyes off Shido. "…What did you say?"

He didn't know what kind of information she'd just heard, but the look on her face abruptly grew stern.

"Yes. Yes. I understand. I will handle it," she said, and hung up.

After a few seconds of what appeared to be hesitation, she released the Territory binding Shido.

"Whoa?!" It was like his supports had been yanked away. Shido lost his balance and lurched forward.

"You are a fortunate person," Ellen told him, and then ran out of the house without so much as a backward glance.

"Huh?" Shido gaped. "Wh-what the…?"

Left alone in his living room, he stared after her blankly for a time and then finally realized that his own phone was still ringing. He walked over to it and glanced at the screen to see Kotori's name displayed there.

"Hello? Kotori? Listen to this. I just—"

"*What took you so long?! What were you doing?! This is an emergency!*" Kotori thundered.

"Wh-what? I was having my own trouble over here, you know."

"*Whatever. Stay calm and listen to me,*" Kotori said, her voice quite serious.

Shido wanted to grumble, but her unusual manner made him frown instead. "What happened?"

"*Well. You're not going to believe this, but…*" Kotori took a deep breath before continuing. "*An artificial satellite is going to fall on Tengu in maybe half an hour.*"

Chapter 10
Fall Down

"Tsk!" Ellen clicked her tongue in annoyance, contracted her Territory, and raced across the ground at incredible speed. Passersby opened their eyes wide in total shock as she zipped past, but she had no time to deal with that now. She focused her entire body and soul on her destination and ran.

Her route was east—the direction of the hotel where Westcott was staying.

At this speed, the time required to arrive there would be approximately thirty minutes. She didn't know the precise time of impact, but considering the fact that they would also have to get away from Tengu once she reached the hotel, she definitely didn't have the luxury of dawdling.

"I have no other choice." Ellen narrowed her eyes and issued orders in her mind.

Instantly, her body shone with a pale light and was equipped in a millisecond with the platinum CR unit Pendragon. Using this, she deployed a Territory with a far greater concentration of magic than what she had been using a few seconds ago.

When she kicked off the ground, the thrusters attached to the rear of the unit fired, and she danced high up into the air. She carved out a straight line toward her target.

And then a call came in over the earpiece equipped in the unit.

"E-Executive Leader Mathers! What on earth is happening?!"

It was one of the subordinates she'd put on standby outside the Itsuka home. She was no doubt surprised because Ellen had suddenly come running from the house.

Keeping her eyes forward and maintaining her speed, Ellen replied, "It's an emergency. Currently, DSA-IV, a decommissioned satellite, is dropping toward the city of Tengu. And it's…"

She continued to explain, and her subordinate cried out, stunned.

"Wha…?! However much we want to remove the Spirits, why would they…?! And the idea that you would not be informed of such a mission—"

"No, the target is not a Spirit. It's Ike." Ellen was quick to correct her subordinate.

"Hah?! M-MD Westcott?! Wh-what do you mean?!" her subordinate cried out in surprise.

Well, that was only natural. The DEM sword was being turned on its top leader.

"I received a message earlier from the head office. The executives who moved to dismiss Ike are apparently out of control." Ellen clicked her tongue. She knew that instead of taking their arms that day, she should have taken their heads.

In the end, right before they were about to carry out the mission, one of those executives had apparently leaked the information to the second enforcement division out of fear of Westcott. She wouldn't say that this decision wasn't a clever one. But if he was going to turn traitor, she would've liked him to come to that decision a little sooner. Ellen had a distinct desire to chew the man out.

That said, however, this was not the time for that. She had to secure Westcott immediately and take him as far away as possible.

"I'm on my way to Ike now. All of you, please withdraw so that you are well outside the impact zone. If you detect a Spirit signal in the area after impact or there are any Spirits caught in the explosion, please collect their Sefirahs."

"*R-roger,*" her subordinate replied, and then cut the connection.

Ellen didn't expect much to come from her request about the Spirits. Given that Ratatoskr had gotten their claws into them, the organization would detect DSA-IV before entering the danger zone and secure any Spirits in the area to move them to safety. Most likely, Shido Itsuka's phone ringing at the house had been a call to inform him of this.

"…!"

While she was racing across the sky, Ellen's eyebrows jumped up.

The reason was simple.

Vwnnnnnnnnnnnnnnnnnnnnnnnnnnnmmmmm.

An earsplitting alarm had begun to ring in the area.

"The spacequake alarm… Impossible. A Spirit?" she murmured, but then quickly hit upon another possibility.

If they were to drop something like a satellite on a Japanese city just because Westcott was in the way, regardless of powerful DEM might have been, there would have been consequences. That would make it impossible for the board to take over the company as intended.

Essentially, the board intended to blame the imminent disaster on a spacequake. There was a certain cold logic to the idea.

"I will not allow it." Ellen gritted her teeth and headed toward Westcott at maximum speed.

Not long after Ellen left his house, the spacequake alarm started to sound, and Shido heard the residents in the area begin to evacuate.

"A spacequake alarm?! *Now*?!" He looked out the window in surprise.

"*No, that's not it,*" Kotori said to him over the phone. "*We're not registering any spacequake fluctuations in the area. This is either a malfunction with the most miraculous timing, or the work of someone who wants to pin the ensuing damage from the falling satellite on a spacequake.*"

"Pinning it all on a spacequake?" Shido gasped. "But who would—?!"

"*DEM probably*," Kotori said through what sounded like clenched teeth.

But Shido frowned. "H-hang on a second. DEM? It couldn't be them, could it?"

"*You do say the darnedest things, huh? I very much doubt there's another organization out there that could do this or are in the condition of having enough screws loose to actually carry it out.*"

"Oh yeah. Well, that is true…"

Shido went on to explain to Kotori what had just happened to him. How Ellen had been here when he got home. And how she had run out of the house in a panic.

"*Ellen Mathers? That is odd. If this was a plan to take out the Spirits in one go, then there's no way she wouldn't have known about it. And before that even…*" Kotori groaned to herself. But then she no doubt realized that this was not the time for sitting in contemplation. She pulled herself together and continued. "*Anyway! It's definitely dangerous for you to stay where you are. Fraxinus will pick you up, so go outside.*"

"R-right." He nodded. "What about Tohka and them?"

"*No need to worry. They're getting ready now to leave the underground facility. Once we grab you, we'll head over there.*"

"Okay. So then—" Shido was about to respond when he stopped and cocked his head to one side. "'Leave'? Isn't that facility strong enough to act as a shelter?"

Kotori paused before responding. "*It is. It'll almost certainly hold up fine against anything up to a B-rank spacequake.*"

"Hang on. Then—"

"*Normally, there'd be no problem. But something's worrying me,*" she said.

"Worrying you?" he asked.

"*Mm-hmm. It's faint, but we've detected a magic signal from that satellite.*"

Shido frowned. "S-so what does that mean?"

"*I don't know yet. But it's hard to imagine that DEM would forcibly down the remains of your run-of-the-mill satellite. It might even be possible that they're punching through the atmosphere somehow. We have to prepare for the worst case."*

"The...worst case," he repeated slowly.

"Yes. The shelters that were deployed around the world thirty years ago were mainly envisioned with spacequake damage in mind. And because the majority of spacequakes are measured above ground, above sea, and in the air, the idea is that there's a good chance you can avoid injury just by hiding underground. But," Kotori said, continuing, *"things are different in this case."*

"So you're saying if that satellite fell directly onto a shelter, the people inside would be doomed?!" Shido cried.

"I told you, I don't know the details yet. But you have to understand that this is a possibility."

"Wh-what the hell?!" Shido shouted, clenching his hands into fists. "They'd do all this just to get at the Spirits! That's...!"

Kotori groaned again. *"We don't know that yet."*

"Huh?"

"DEM knows we have an airship," she explained. *"I find it hard to believe they would use a method this uncertain if they were targeting a Spirit."*

"S-so then what is this about?" he asked.

"I can't say anything at present. Either the people at the top are idiots with poor judgment, or they've finally completely lost it. Or they have some other objective."

"'Objective'..." Shido swallowed hard. What "objective" was worth achieving at the costs of potentially tens of thousands of victims?

"I get how you feel, but you have to hurry," Kotori said impatiently. *"While we're here chewing the fat, we're losing time before impact."*

But Shido didn't move. "H-hold up a minute. Can't we do something?! I mean, even if *we* make it, the people of the city will—"

"Hear me out," Kotori said sharply, cutting him off. *"I mean, I'm not over here thinking we should watch everyone die. We've already got a plan."*

"R-really?!"

"*Yes. It's simple. Before the satellite crashes, we shoot it down with Fraxinus's weapons. Then even if the explosive magic is activated, there might be blowback and chunks of satellite hitting the ground, but the shelters underground should be safe... Above ground might be a hell of a sight, though, but that'd be the same as with a spacequake, and we're golden if people are just grateful for their lives at least. The SDF recovery division will have to pick up the pieces for us after that.*"

"I get it." Shido nodded. "In that case!"

"*So you're on board?*" Kotori asked. "*Then get a move on.*"

"Right!" He ended the call and headed for the front door. When he crouched down to put his shoes on, something fell out of his pocket with a *tunk*.

"Hmm?" He looked down to see a Chupa Chups in a red wrapper. The one that Natsumi-Kotori had dropped in the underground facility.

"Oh."

The moment he saw it, Shido had a sudden thought. For a few seconds, he gaped, bewildered, and the world around him froze.

Right. He'd forgotten. His neighbors were all evacuating to underground shelters because of the spacequake alarm. And they would all be saved if *Fraxinus*'s attack on the satellite succeeded.

But there might have been just one person who remained above ground, having recently fled from a secure facility.

Shido stopped in the entryway, and his phone began to chirp again. When he pressed the ANSWER button, he heard Kotori's annoyed voice.

"*Come on. What're you doing, Shido? We don't have time—*"

"Kotori," he said simply.

Kotori cut her impatient speech short. Perhaps picking up on something from Shido's tone, she asked dubiously, "*What? Something going on?*"

"Yeah. I have a favor to ask," he said. "Could you go get Tohka and them first?"

"*Huh? Why? Ohhh, is it like get them to safety before you? You don't have to worry. We can definitely grab everyone.*"

"No. There's something down here I still have to do."

"*What?!*" she cried out angrily. "*Do you not get that this is an emergency?! I don't know what this thing you have to do is, but your life comes first! Of all the—*"

"It's Natsumi."

"*…!*" Kotori was at a loss for words.

"You haven't found her yet, right?" he said.

If she was still above ground, she was in serious trouble.

A normal person would run for a shelter when the spacequake alarm went off. That was only natural. But he didn't know whether or not the Spirit Natsumi would obey that alarm. He couldn't imagine that she would be particularly eager to go into an underground shelter when she'd been locked up in an underground facility.

"*That's…,*" Kotori protested. "*But Natsumi's no fool! Shelters and all that aside, it's possible she's long gone from this place. And even if there's an explosion and chunks of satellite start raining down, she's a Spirit, okay?! She should be able to avoid all that stuff, no problem!*"

"Maybe," Shido agreed. "But she's still not completely healed from Ellen's attack. The worst case is possible here."

"*…*" Kotori groaned faintly before falling entirely silent.

"Please," he begged her over the phone. "Let me look for Natsumi until the very last minute? It might be pointless. Actually, it's almost guaranteed to be pointless. But given that Natsumi might be in danger, I can't just sit back and watch," he finished, clenching his hands into fists.

Kotori was silent for a while.

"*Aaagh,*" she groaned finally in exasperation. "*Fine. Or more like, you wouldn't listen even if I did tell you not to.*"

"Kotori!" His heart leaped in gratitude.

"*But!*" she cautioned. "*You've only got until we're ready to attack. I can't allow you to search any longer than that. And you put in your earpiece so I can contact you on the fly.*"

"Okay, got it." He nodded.

"*Then go. I'll have the rest of the autonomous cameras searching for Natsumi, too. Don't get your hopes up, though.*"

"Roger! Kotori!"

"*What?*"

"Thanks," he said simply, and Kotori sniffed over the telephone line.

"*I could say the same to you. I almost overlooked something import-ant in the rush. Go get her, Shido.*"

Shido nodded and picked up the Chupa Chups he'd dropped in the hallway before leaving the house.

His neighbors had mostly evacuated by now; he saw basically no one on the road. It was a curious silence with just the air of people having recently been there lingering. He had walked through more than one deserted area in order to talk with a Spirit, but no matter how many times he experienced this strange isolation, he could never enjoy the bizarre feel of it.

But this was no time to be wondering about this. As he ran, Shido took a deep breath and called out loudly, "Natsumiii!!"

His voice echoed throughout the unnaturally quiet neighborhood. But of course, he got no response.

He'd expected that, though. Heedless, he kept shouting:

"If you're here, answer me! Chunks of satellite are going to be hitting this area really soon! It's dangerous to stay here! We have to hurry and evacuate! Just for a bit's okay! Come with me! I won't lock you up in some room or anything! Once it's all over, you can go wherever you want! Please!"

Shido's shouts reverberated through the streets of the residential area and faded away. And there was, naturally, no answer.

But he didn't believe his doing this was a waste of time.

He didn't know where Natsumi was. Maybe Kotori was right, and she had already run off to some other place. Or maybe she had mixed in with the residents of the neighborhood and slipped into an under-ground shelter.

But if she was still above ground and in the city of Tengu, then he had to assume it was at least somewhat likely that she was hiding somewhere, watching him in order to get back at him for locking her up underground.

Betting on that slim chance, he kept yelling:

"It's fine if you don't like me! Just go hide in a shelter with the other people or get out of town as fast as you can! Or even...you could escape to the parallel world! But you're in danger if you stay here! Please! You have to get out of here!"

Shouting at the top of his lungs while running forced a serious burden on his respiratory system. He hadn't gone any real distance, but his lungs ached, and he was having trouble breathing.

But he didn't stop. Natsumi might have been hiding somewhere nearby.

Shido took another deep breath to call out and have his voice reach her.

"Natsumi! Please! If you can hear me, answer me!" Shido cried out for the nth time as he raced through the deserted city.

"..." Natsumi listened silently.

Most likely, Shido thought that the escaped Natsumi was still in this area and that she was somewhere she could observe him.

And he was exactly right.

"Natsumi! Natsumi! Are you there?! Natsumi!" he called, his voice hoarse, and he was panting hard. He was a pathetic sight.

But Shido didn't stop yelling. He tripped over a rock and nearly fell, but he quickly pulled himself back up and started to shout Natsumi's name once more.

"Why would you do this?" Natsumi nearly said, and stopped herself just in time.

It wasn't that she thought Shido would figure out where she was if she spoke. It was simply that even without speaking the words, she knew the answer.

Why?

It was obviously to save her.

Debris from a satellite was going to fall in this area. Most likely,

Shido was telling the truth. From what she'd seen of the people in the area evacuating, there was no doubt that some kind of disaster was on the way.

Of course, if it was just that, she could imagine that the organization backing Shido and his friends was sounding the alarm to draw her out. But the phone call between Shido and Kotori that she'd overheard before ruled that out.

Shido had stayed in the city alone, exposing himself to danger for the sole reason that Natsumi might have still been around.

"Ungh…"

When she had this thought, that curious feeling spread through her chest again. Warm, fuzzy, swirly, spinny, dizzy. Sick.

When Natsumi had first manifested silently in this world, not a soul had looked at her. And she had hated that so, so much. She had wanted someone to talk to her, pay attention to her, accept her so badly that she could hardly stand it. So she had remade herself with the power of Haniel.

Everyone was nice to Natsumi when she transformed into a beautiful young woman. Everyone fawned over her and did whatever she asked.

But after a few rounds of this, Natsumi's heart was still unsatisfied.

In the end, no one was actually looking at her. In the end, no one was actually accepting her. The more they cozied up to her, the stronger that feeling got.

But the person Shido was looking for now was the real Natsumi no one else had accepted. He was trying to find the Natsumi whom everyone had ignored.

"…!"

She flashed back to everything that had happened so far. Shido and the others rescuing her when Ellen attacked her. Him and his friends giving her a makeover. Making her think she was cute. Accepting her the way she was.

"No way. I…" She didn't need to think about it any longer.

Natsumi didn't want Shido to die.

The fact that he'd seen her secret had at some point stopped mattering without her realizing it. What was more important now was that she had someone who really saw her, a fact that delighted her beyond words.

"Natsumi!"

"...!"

He called her name, and for a second, she nearly cried out in response.

It wouldn't have been a big deal if she had spoken up. Shido would have surely found her. They could have escaped to some place safe together.

But Natsumi didn't know what to do with these feelings she was experiencing for the first time.

"I-it's okay. You're okay," she murmured, too quietly for Shido to notice.

Whatever else, Shido would evacuate when chunks of satellite started to fall. In the worst case, whatever organization he belonged to would definitely pick him up or something like when they saved Natsumi.

Chanting "It's okay, you're okay" as if to reassure herself, Natsumi prayed that Shido would give up his search for her right this second and evacuate to a safe place.

"Tohka and the other Spirits have been recovered from the D3 underground facility!"

"Recovery of thirteen accompanying personnel complete!"

"Closing facility bulkheads via remote operation!"

Approximately twenty minutes after accepting Shido's proposal and setting out into the deserted city, Kotori listened to her crew's reports on the bridge, then spoke. "Excellent. What's Shido's current location?"

"Shido is currently running north along the main street in Sanchome. It appears he is heading toward the high school."

"Any sign of Natsumi on the cameras?" Kotori asked.

"Unfortunately, we have no confirmed sightings," a member of her crew replied.

"I see," she answered briefly. She had never thought they would find Natsumi that easily anyway, not when she had the power of transformation.

"Commander! The satellite has begun to fall!" Minowa cried out from the lower deck just as Kotori was about to give her next order, and a red icon on the monitor began to flash.

Normally, when an artificial satellite fell, it gradually strayed from its orbit and slowly lost altitude as it spun around the earth, due to the effects of air friction and gravity, before plunging into the atmosphere and burning up.

But the icon displayed on the monitor was dropping straight toward the earth from its orbit, as if being yanking down by a vertical rope. This was clearly out of the ordinary.

"Here we go." Kotori licked her lips, threw a hand up, and barked orders at the crew. "Calculate estimated point of impact now! Activate AR-008 numbers three through five and be ready to fire Mistilteinn at any moment! After recovering Shido, we move to the intercept point and destroy the target!"

Normally, it would have been extremely difficult to accurately predict the point of impact for a falling satellite. But with the calculation capabilities of the AI installed in *Fraxinus*, it was possible to estimate a location within a margin of a few kilometers. All the more so if it was dropping straight down as if shooting toward a target.

"Roger! AR-008: three, four, five, magic generation start!"

"We have the estimated point of impact! The satellite is aimed at an area in east Tengu!" Mikimoto reported.

Kotori clicked her tongue. "Tch! Surprisingly close to Shido's location."

The transporter device on *Fraxinus* could only be used when the ship was directly above the target with no obstacles blocking that line of sight. In other words, if they were going to collect someone from the ground, they had to position themselves directly above that someone.

That said, however, given that there was the risk that the explosive magic would activate at the same time as they intercepted the satellite, it wasn't particularly advisable for *Fraxinus* to get too close to the target. After picking up Shido near the predicted impact location, they would have to move away from that point once more and prepare to intercept the satellite.

"How much time do we have to get away after recovering Shido?" Kotori demanded.

"Approximately...five minutes and thirty seconds!" a crew member replied.

"Not much time considering preparation to intercept." Kotori bit her lip. "Let's hurry it up."

"Yes, sir!"

The low rumble of motors engaging echoed through the airship, and *Fraxinus* began to move from its fixed position in the air.

Kotori confirmed this before issuing another order. "Open a line with Shido."

"Roger." Nakatsugawa tapped at his console.

On one side of the monitor, a video feed of Shido running through town searching for Natsumi was displayed.

She brought the mic at hand to her mouth and sent her voice to Shido's earpiece. "Shido, can you hear me?"

The Shido on the screen looked up and stopped.

"*Y-yeah...I can...hear you...,*" Shido replied, pressing a finger to his earpiece as he panted for breath. His voice was raspy like when he had a cold. It appeared he'd been calling out to Natsumi nonstop while running.

Seeing him like this made her hesitate to continue. But she couldn't let him keep looking for Natsumi. She shook her head slightly to get herself back on track and spoke into the mic. "Sorry, but time's up. We're coming to get you, so stay put."

"Wha...?!" he said pleadingly. "*All...ready...?! Please, just a little more—*"

"No. You promised."

"*B-but...*"

Kotori bit into her Chupa Chups with a *crack*. "Don't make me tell you again. You have to include yourself on the list of the lives you're trying to save."

Shido fell silent for a moment before letting out a short sigh. "*Fine. Sorry for being selfish.*"

"No probs. Used to it," Kotori said, waving it away with a hand, and turned her eyes to the monitor again.

In that instant, a buzzer to announce an emergency situation began to sound over the speakers set up on the bridge.

"What?!"

"I-it's..." A crew member from the lower deck gasped. "The speed of the satellite's descent is increasing dramatically!"

"What did you say?!" Kotori frowned as the satellite in question was displayed on the monitor. A square body with solar panels on both sides. Some kind of awkward round object was affixed to the top, half embedded in it. This addition appeared to be acting as makeshift thrusters. This was clearly no ordinary satellite.

"Ngh. What is *that*?!" Kotori's eyes flew open, and a bead of sweat ran down her cheek. Did this mean they wanted the scale of damage upon impact to be bigger? Or had they anticipated *Fraxinus* being in the air above Tengu and were on guard against interception?

Either way, there was no doubt that this was not a happy situation for Kotori and her crew. Slamming a fist down on the armrest of her captain's chair, she stood up and yelled down to the lower deck of the bridge. "Update the estimated arrival now! How much time do we have?!"

"I've got the new estimate!" came a call from below. "W-with these numbers, unless we immediately move to intercept, we'll be too late!"

"Ngh!" Kotori screwed her face up into a scowl. But she set her mind to work immediately and calmly assessed what it was she had to do in the moment.

"Sorry, Shido," she said. "Change of plans."

"Huh?"

"We can't come pick you up. But if we intercept the satellite, the damage shouldn't reach below ground. Evacuate right now to the nearest shelter."

"Okay, got it. Don't worry about me. You just take care of this," Shido replied without asking any further questions. He had likely guessed at the situation from Kotori's tone.

Kotori kept her voice from shaking as she said, "I will," and then disconnected.

"C-Commander?" a crew member asked hesitantly.

"No problem here," she said. "Let's hurry and get ready to intercept. We are going to take this thing down."

"R-roger!" the crew shouted, and got to work.

Fraxinus changed course and headed toward the estimated location of impact.

"Ngh." Kotori gritted her teeth and balled her hands into fists.

She had made the right decision here. If she prioritized picking up Shido, *Fraxinus* wouldn't be able to intercept the satellite, and as a result, an enormous number of people would lose their lives. But...

"Commander!"

After she'd been lost in thought for some unknown amount of time, Shiizaki's voice pulled her out of her reverie.

"We have arrived at the point of impact!"

"The target will pass the designated point in thirty seconds!"

"AR-008 magic generation complete! We are ready to go!"

The voices of the crew reverberated on the bridge. Kotori shook her head to clear away any extraneous thoughts and then stared at the monitor.

She started to count down in her mind along with the timer displayed in a corner of the monitor, and the moment the target came onto the screen, she cried out, "Mistilteinn! Fire!"

An incredible stream of magic jetted out from *Fraxinus*'s armaments.

The vast amount of magic produced by the large Realizers equipped on the airship was sucked toward the target displayed in the center of the screen.

Their timing was perfect. There was even one crew member who struck a victorious pose before the hit was confirmed.

However.

"Wha...?!" Kotori cried out in confusion, a look of disbelief on her face.

But this, too, was only to be expected. The focused beam of magic had twisted the slightest bit when it was on the verge of touching the target and merely pierced a solar panel and part of the thruster before disappearing into the sky.

The satellite continued to fall even as it wobbled, bouncing back from the magic gun, as if pulled down by gravity.

"Wh-what was that?!" Kotori shouted.

"A Territory...most likely." It was Kannazuki standing next to her captain's chair who replied thoughtfully, a chin on his hand.

"A Territory?!" Kotori cried, as she noticed a suspicious point on the satellite on the screen.

A familiar face was peeking out from inside the round object that had been shot through by Mistilteinn.

"That's...a Bandersnatch?!"

DEM's mechanical doll, Bandersnatch. More precisely, this was a device that closely resembled that doll, an autonomous DEM weapon that could use a Realizer to deploy a Territory without the intervention of a Wizard.

It had affixed itself to the satellite.

"I never imagined...!" Seeing this, Kotori understood the intent of this device in an instant.

DEM had likely launched a customized Bandersnatch from the ground and had it dock with a satellite scheduled for decommissioning. And although the satellite would have been orbiting at tremendous speed, a machine equipped with a Realizer could have indeed caught it.

And the fact that the Bandersnatch was attached to the satellite meant that it would be possible to deploy a Territory around it.

"So that's it, then. That has to be why the satellite made it through the atmosphere without a scratch!" Kotori clicked her tongue in annoyance, then heard Reine fiddling with her console.

"…This is not good. The impact from a satellite this size falling while maintaining its mass, the high-level DEM explosive magic, and the Territory of a Bandersnatch to amplify everything else…"

There was the sound of keys clacking, and then numbers were displayed on the screen.

"…I don't know the exact numbers, so these are just rough estimates," Reine said. "But I doubt the impact would be less than that of a tactical nuclear weapon."

"…!!" Kotori gasped. She thought she'd envisioned the worst-case scenario, but this situation far surpassed anything she'd imagined. If this thing dropped, the city of Tengu itself would be vaporized.

In the midst of all this, Kannazuki alone was calm, stroking his jaw with a complicated look on his face. "It's curious, isn't it?"

"Wh-what is?" Kotori demanded.

"Oh, I simply find it hard to believe that the Territory generated by a Realizer of the level equipped on a Bandersnatch could knock Mistilteinn off course," he responded.

"So then what exactly—?" Kotori started. "No, whatever. Right now, taking that thing out comes first! Regenerate magic! We have to do something before that satellite hits— Eeah?!"

The bridge of *Fraxinus* rocked from side to side.

"What the—?!" Kotori cried.

"A-an attack!" came the crew report. "Territory has shrunk by fifteen percent!"

"An attack?" She gasped.

"I've got video!" Minowa cried out, while a video feed of the sky was displayed on the monitor. Who knew when it had appeared, but floating there was an airship even more enormous than *Fraxinus*. The hull was composed of straight lines, and yet it had a somehow organic form to it. And Kotori could see in it an unsettling element shared with DEM weaponry.

"Is that...DEM's?!" she cried. "Ngh. So that's what's knocked our shot off course."

Kotori gritted her teeth in frustration. Most likely, Ratatoskr's attempted interception mission had been anticipated.

She didn't know the detailed performance specs of the enemy ship, but it was clear that it had a Territory able to deflect Mistilteinn and the ability to generate this Territory at random points. Until the *Fraxinus* did something about this enemy ship, they wouldn't be able to shoot down the satellite. But if they took on the ship, the satellite would crash into the ground before they had the chance to stop it.

"Commander!" her crew called out, a shiver of fear coloring their expressions. This result here was easy to picture.

However.

Kotori sighed with the utmost calm and sat back down heavily in her captain's chair. "Kannazuki, you handle this. We'll use Gungnir."

Her crew visibly flinched.

"...Are you sure, Kotori?" came Reine's voice from the lower deck.

"Yes. I'm not saying we'll go whole hog or anything. Shido can't exactly lose his power of recovery now, after all," Kotori replied, and looked at her second in command. "You better not miss, Kannazuki."

"I will take care of everything," Kannazuki said, still standing tall.

Kotori nodded, satisfied, and set her palm down on an authentication device affixed to the edge of her console.

The captain's chair, where she sat, slid downward like it was being swallowed up by the floor, and a few seconds later, Kotori came out into a circular space about six meters across.

Because events outside were projected onto the smoothly curving wall in real time, she had the sensation that she was floating in space.

But Kotori couldn't afford to simply enjoy a lighthearted walk through the air at the moment. She jumped down from her captain's chair, stood in the center of the circle, and breathed deeply to calm her mind.

"Now, shall we begin our battle?"

The sensation of reeling in a thin thread from inside the cage of her consciousness. The image of incandescent flames enveloping her body.

Eventually, this picture was imbued with reality, and flames had no sooner started to swirl around Kotori than they were forming a fantastic robe. The fire crawled up her hair to manifest demon-like horns on the sides of her head.

Astral Dress. The absolute armor covering a Spirit.

Kotori's Spirit powers had been sealed by Shido in the past, but by controlling her own mental state, she could cause that power to flow back from him at will.

That said, however, if she took 100 percent of the power back, there was the danger of it eating into her very self. By securing a fixed amount of her power, she closed the mental path and maintained a limited Astral Dress.

"Camael," she said quietly, and the flames concentrated in her hand to transform into an enormous battle-ax.

In that moment, an explosion echoed from somewhere, and the airship rocked slightly.

They had probably suffered a hit from the enemy ship. It seemed that they were still defended by a Protect Territory, but if she dawdled here, *Fraxinus* might take some serious damage before they could bring down the satellite.

Brandishing Camael, Kotori spoke. "Megiddo!"

Camael stretched out into a cylindrical shape and equipped itself neatly on Kotori's arm. It looked almost like a cannon. A massive weapon affixed to her right arm, seeming very out of place on Kotori's small body.

And at the same time, a device like a large connector descended before her. When Kotori touched the end of Camael to it, there was a quiet electronic *beep*, and Camael and the device were firmly connected.

"Here we go, Kannazuki," she said.

"Any time you're ready." She heard Kannazuki's voice in response over the speaker.

If the concentrated-magic weapon Mistilteinn could be knocked aside, then they had only one course of action left to them. It was plain and simple. They had to attack with even greater power.

The Spirit power weapon, Gungnir.

Just as its name implied, this was the most powerful weapon on *Fraxinus*. It converted the power of a Spirit, amplified it, and released a lethal blow.

Lingering bits of Spirit power crackled like sparks around her body as Kotori narrowed her eyes sharply and shouted, "Now! Spirit power weapon Gungnir!"

"Fire!"

At the same time as Kannazuki's voice rang out over the speaker, a beam of Spirit power was launched from the enormous weapon in the center of *Fraxinus*.

This was not on the level of a laser or a beam. If it had to be put into words—a pillar. A giant pillar of light made of concentrated Spirit power stretched out in a straight line between *Fraxinus* and the satellite.

What on earth would happen to the target if it was struck by this mass of Spirit power? This would soon be demonstrated with an unparalleled real-world example.

The blow hit the satellite dead-on, and the Territory around it flared to life to try and knock it off course once again. But Gungnir pushed back against this meager defense and annihilated the satellite falling toward Tengu, leaving not a trace of it behind.

Explosive magic. Countless fragments. They'd vaporized the satellite without a trace of the damage they'd anticipated with this single, simple super–high output blow.

"Target destroyed! We have succeeded!" The voice of her crew member came through the speaker, and Kotori slumped to her knees.

"Haah… Haah…"

A slight headache and some dizziness overcame her. Perhaps because she had handled the power of a Spirit, albeit only part of it, a dubious destructive urge started to flicker to life like a fire in her heart.

This was the biggest reason that they couldn't often use the absolute force of Gungnir. If Kotori's mind was swallowed up by that destructive urge, Kotori herself would become a threat to *Fraxinus*. Because of this, they could only risk firing this weapon at truly do-or-die moments.

Breathing deeply, Kotori waved her Angel away, released her Astral Dress, and sat back on the floor. And then she spoke to her crew on the bridge.

"Nice work. But we can't slow down now. The enemy ship—"

A shrill emergency alarm rang out suddenly, as if to interrupt her.

"What is it?!" she cried. "Is the enemy coming at us with something new?!"

"*N-no! That's not it! I-it's—,*" a crew member cried, as a radar image was displayed in part of the screen showing the scene in the sky.

She looked at the signal shown there and gasped. "Wha...? There's...*another* satellite?!"

Yes. A signal exactly like the one they'd just destroyed had appeared in the sky above *Fraxinus* once more.

"It can't be... The one just now was a decoy?!" Kotori screwed up her face in annoyance.

Most likely, the enemy had assumed that they would have an airship and a means of taking down the satellite, and thus, they had readied a number of satellites right from the start.

Kotori gritted her teeth, pressed her hands against her thighs, and stood up. "If that's how they want it! We'll just go again!"

"*...No, you can't. The burden of multiple Gungnirs is too much for you and for* Fraxinus," Reine said quietly, as Kotori held up a hand to manifest her Angel once more.

There was another explosion, and the airship was rocked more powerfully than before.

"Ngh!" Kotori groaned.

The enemy attacks were increasing in ferocity. It was too dangerous to stay on the defensive like this. They needed to shift to counterattacking immediately or take evasive action.

This was the worst situation she could think of. Even though a second satellite was being dropped toward the ground, they couldn't fire Gungnir again, and they couldn't break through that airship's Territory with the output of Mistilteinn. Actually, even before that, if they tried to go hard on attacking the satellite, *Fraxinus* might be put down before they could manage that.

"What exactly are we—?" For a second or two, Kotori struggled to come to a decision, and over the speaker, she heard the door to the bridge opening.

"*Mm... Wh-what's going on?*" Tohka said in confusion, perhaps seeing the uproar on the bridge, the enemy ship shown on the monitor, and the video of the second satellite dropping.

Apparently, she and the others secured earlier had stepped onto the bridge.

"*Uh. Um... What is that...?*"

"*Ooh-hoo! Looks like a real jam!*"

"*Keh-keh! Pathetic. To think that you would be disconcerted at a mere nothing!*"

"*Conformity. You should remain calm.*"

"*Hmm? That videoooo, that's the satellite you were talking about, right? It kind of... I feel like it's still faaaalling?*"

Following Tohka onto the bridge, Yoshino, Yoshinon, Kaguya, Yuzuru, and Miku spoke one after the other.

"E-everyone!" Kotori cried out, her eyes flying open.

"*Kotori?*" Tohka replied doubtfully. "*Where are you? I don't see Shido, either. Where...?*"

Kotori gasped unconsciously.

Perhaps sensing something in Kotori's reaction, Tohka's face grew somewhat sterner. "*Kotori, what happened? Tell us. Can we help at all?*"

"...!" Kotori wordlessly clenched her jaw. The Spirits were to be protected at all costs. Even by accident, she couldn't send them to the dangerous surface.

But Shido was on the surface.

If he knew that the satellite was still falling toward the ground,

Shido, that softhearted big brother of hers, would without a doubt stand against it.

Commander and little sister.

Caught in between those two positions, Kotori half-unconsciously opened her mouth.

"Please... All of you. That idiot... My only big brother... You have to save him!"

"Time's up...huh?" After disconnecting from the call with Kotori, Shido lowered his eyes and squeezed his hands into fists.

The idea of ignoring Kotori's order to evacuate and keep looking for Natsumi flitted through his mind. Even if the blowback and satellite chunks did rain down and seriously injure him, he would be able to recover, given that he had Kotori's blessing—just as long as he didn't die instantly.

But when he thought about this, Kotori's words came back to life in the back of his mind.

"You have to include yourself on the list of the lives you're trying to save."

"Right. Sorry, Kotori," Shido said, rethinking things, and lifted his face.

He'd run around shouting at the top of his lungs for this long. If Natsumi was watching him, then she would have realized the situation was dire and run off already. All he could do now was pray that this assumption was true.

He let his gaze roam and searched for a nearby public shelter. When the spacequake alarm order was issued, electronic markers and notice boards popped up to indicate the route to the nearest shelter.

Once he had confirmed which way he needed to go, he called out loudly to the area once more, "Natsumi! I'm evacuating to an underground shelter! If you don't know where a shelter is, you can follow me!"

There was…no response, of course.

"Okay?!"

Shido prayed his voice would reach Natsumi and ran toward the shelter.

Because he'd been running around looking for Natsumi, his breathing was labored, and his feet throbbed. But he couldn't just stop. He didn't know how much time he had left, but if Kotori and *Fraxinus* had smashed the satellite, then there would be an explosion pretty soon. He had to make it to a shelter before that. And if Natsumi was secretly following him, she would get caught up in the explosion, too.

Forcing his body forward when it wanted to do nothing other than stop, he somehow managed to reach the closest shelter.

Because a fair bit of time had passed since the alarm went off, the main entrance was already closed. But public shelters like this were generally built with an emergency entrance for stragglers like Shido. He turned his feet in that direction.

"*Phew…* Made it." Standing in front of the emergency entrance, Shido breathed a sigh of relief and looked behind him. "Natsumi! It's here! You can come in secret! Before the pieces start to fall!"

He raised his chin so that his voice would carry to make his last plea.

However.

"Huh…?" Shido froze.

And the reason for that was simple. When he lifted his face, he caught sight of a small shadow of something in a break in the clouds.

"That's…" His eyes widened for a moment, but then he realized what it actually was. The satellite Kotori had been talking about.

"Uh, this has to be a joke?" His voice shook.

And of course it did. Because the thing falling toward the city of Tengu at that moment was not a collection of tiny bits and pieces—it was a massive hunk of steel.

If the satellite hit the ground like that, the shelters in the area wouldn't make it out unscathed. He recalled what Kotori had said before and felt something cold spread through his stomach.

It couldn't be. Had *Fraxinus* failed to shoot it down?! He hurriedly raised his voice at his earpiece. "Kotori! Hey! Kotori! What the hell's going on?!"

He heard a static-filled voice in response.

"Shido?! An enemy airship… Shot failed…but now—"

"Huh?! Wh-what did you say?!" he asked, but only heard something like an explosion before the earpiece went dead.

He didn't know the details. But he could see at least that something irregular had happened in the air.

The clumsy black silhouette was slowly but surely growing larger.

"Dammit!" he shouted, and started running away instead of entering the shelter.

There was no point in fleeing to the shelter if the satellite was going to crash without being smashed first. The impact and the explosive magic would vaporize the whole area, and the people in the shelters would die.

Tonomachi, Ai-Mai-Mii, and the rest of his classmates, his homeroom teacher Tama, the neighbors he said hello to in the mornings, the shopkeepers who were always so nice to him… Too many lives to count would vanish in an instant.

"I can't…let that happen!" he cried, as he glared at the sky and raced to a spot directly below the satellite.

He was under no delusion that he alone could do anything about such an enormous satellite. But there was no one else on the ground who could act at the moment. If Shido gave up, then his fear of everyone losing their lives would become fact. He couldn't allow that.

"…!"

That said, however, the speed of the satellite's descent was tremendous. It was growing more massive before his eyes, and Shido could take in the entirety of it now.

"Ngh!" He gritted his teeth as he ran.

It was hopeless. Even if he did make it to the point where the satellite would hit, it would only end with the city being blown away along with Shido.

Power.

He needed enough power to quell with one blow the manifestation of despair that was dropping through the sky.

But Shido was human. Just another regular—although he'd walked a checkered path in life so maybe this adjective wasn't totally accurate—human being. Normally, he wouldn't have had power like that.

But. If it wasn't Shido's. If it was the power of Spirits borrowed by Shido.

"Please… I'm all we've got! Lend me your strength!" he shouted, and thrust his right hand out. As if reaching for some invisible something. Or to grab hold of something.

In his mind, he pictured only his desire to save everyone.

"Please… Sandalphon!"

A dazzling light filled his field of vision, and he felt something in his right hand.

When the light blinding him died away, he found a faintly glowing, enormous sword had appeared in his hand.

The Angel Sandalphon. The absolute sword Tohka possessed.

"I did it!" he cried out unconsciously. He'd managed to manifest this Angel a few times before, but this was the first time he'd done it of his own will like this.

"Now I can…!" Shido's gaze grew sharper as he stopped and looked up at the falling satellite, readying Sandalphon in both hands.

He exhaled steadily and calmed his mind. He banished all extraneous thought and concentrated solely on protecting the people on the ground.

And then Shido brandished Sandalphon.

"Haaaaaaaaaaaaah!"

Light spilled from Sandalphon, extending into the sky, following the line of Shido's blade. An absolute blow from a powerful Angel. Whatever Territory the enemy might have deployed, it would be easily crushed in the face of an attack by an Angel.

However.

"Wha…?!" Shido's eyes grew round as saucers.

The attack he had launched twisted unnaturally as it approached the satellite and shot out past the target into the sky.

The satellite itself was undamaged. Roaring through the air, it hurtled toward the ground, ready to destroy Tengu.

"Dammit! One more time—"

Shido gritted his teeth and was about to swing Sandalphon a second time. But in that instant, an intense pain raced through his body, and his face twisted up as he fell to one knee.

"Ah! Ngh!"

This was the price for handling this power, the Angel, which was far beyond anything human. Shido's entire body was in tatters after swinging the greatsword just once.

And then an incandescence, like he had been swallowed by a bonfire, enveloped his body. The regenerative power of flames he'd gained through half-forcibly sealing Kotori's powers were healing his body.

"Ngh!"

Anguish colored his face, and he tightened the grip of his right hand to keep from dropping Sandalphon.

But while this was happening, the satellite was still closing in on the ground. If he waited for his body to heal, everything would be over before he could strike again. Shido somehow managed to pull himself to his feet in the middle of this pain and heat, which very nearly made him lose consciousness.

"Ngh. Ah. Ah. Ah…!" He brandished Sandalphon with all his strength. But the satellite was already enormous in his field of vision. The entire city of Tengu would likely be vaporized in the next ten seconds.

"Ah. Aaaaaaaaaah!" Shido swung Sandalphon with everything he had. But with his lack of focus, there was no way he would be able to totally control the Angel. The tip of Sandalphon cut fruitlessly through the air and hit the ground with a *thud.*

But Shido didn't give up. His muscles were torn, cracks riddled his spine, and even though his whole body burned white-hot in order to forcefully heal these injuries, he still didn't let go of Sandalphon.

"I won't...let you!" he cried, bracing his legs, which threatened to give out under him.

If Shido gave up, then in that instant, all those people who had evacuated to the shelters would be killed. He absolutely could never, ever step back and let that happen.

"You...don't! Come down...on...my cityyyyyyyyyyy!"

Shido mustered up every last bit of strength he had and brought Sandalphon down. The sword strike turned into light and stretched out as though sucked into the satellite. But this blow, too, failed to break through the Territory.

"...?!" He gasped.

He felt an abrupt frigid wind blow by, an all-too-sudden chill even on the eve of winter. But he realized soon enough that he knew this particular chill.

"It's..." He tilted his head back to the sky and held his breath.

The satellite had stopped in a position several hundred meters above the ground. Actually, to be more precise, the concentrated wind pressure of an ascending air current and a wall of ice had just barely managed to keep the satellite from firing its thrusters and charging toward the earth.

"Shido!"

He heard a familiar voice from behind and turned his aching body to find Yoshino there clinging to an Angel in the shape of a gigantic rabbit puppet.

"Yoshino." He gasped. "What are you doing here?!"

"Keh-keh! Yoshino is not alone in this."

"Dissatisfaction. I wanted you to see Yuzuru in action."

He heard two more voices from the sky above. The Yamai sisters were floating there, limited Astral Dresses and Angels manifested. It appeared that Yoshino and the Yamais had stopped the fall of the satellite in the nick of time.

"Shido!" Tohka cried.

Followed by Miku's "Daaaarling!"

Both Spirits were clad in dresses of pale light, and Tohka held in her hand a sword of the same shape as the Angel that Shido gripped.

"Tohka...and Miku!" Shido said, surprise coloring his face.

"Mm." Tohka nodded firmly. "Kotori told us you were in trouble, so we got her to send us right away. I'm glad we made it in time."

"Me too. What about Kotori and them?" he asked, and this time, Miku spoke up.

"They're fiiiighting the enemy's airship. Well, I think we're probably okay leaving that to them, though."

It all made sense now. That was likely why *Fraxinus* had failed to destroy the satellite and why his call to them earlier had cut out. He was worried about the airship and its crew, but all he could do was have faith in Kotori. He turned back to Tohka and the others and bowed.

"Thanks. You saved me. To be honest, I thought I was done for."

"What are you talking about? You're the one who saved us, Shido. This doesn't come close to repaying everything you've done for us," Tohka said, and the other Spirits bobbed their heads up and down.

"Gang..." He looked at each of them in turn gratefully.

"Ah...!" Yoshino cried, and the Yamai sisters scowled.

"Keh! What now? This knave has the nerve to increase in power."

"Outrage. I do wish you'd read the room."

Apparently, the customized Bandersnatch fused with the satellite had boosted its thruster output. This seemed like the most likely explanation for why the satellite, which had been forced to a stop in midair, began to slowly approach the ground once more.

Miku threw out both arms and then crossed them in front of her body. "No, thaaaank you!"

A keyboard of light appeared before her as if chasing the trajectory of her hands; a large pipe organ of an Angel manifested behind her.

"Gabriel. March!" Miku shouted, as her slender fingers danced nimbly across the shining keyboard. A stirring song poured out from the Angel, and the wind-slash-ice wall combo pushing back the satellite grew significantly stronger.

"That's...amazing," Yoshino said appreciatively.

"Keh-keh!" Kaguya threw her head back and laughed. "This chanson is indeed excellent. The blood sings, the flesh dances!"

"Vigor. This is a great assist," Yuzuru agreed.

Miku's Angel, Gabriel, could manipulate sound. By playing different songs, it could cause a variety of effects on its target. Those who heard the valiant March would have their mind and body roused, allowing them to wield greater power than normal.

Feeling new strength well up inside his own self, Shido clenched his hands into fists. "All right. So then! Tohka, help me! We're smashing that massive thing. We should be able to do it together!"

He and Tohka both had the same Sandalphon in hand. If they attacked at the same time, they would definitely be able to break through the enemy's Territory.

But Tohka shook her head, a troubled look on her face. "No, we can't."

"We can't?" he asked. "Wh-why can't we?"

"Mm." Tohka's frown grew deeper. "I don't really know why, but Kotori said we can't. I guess it's got this explosive-magic thing that'll activate if it's destroyed. So we have to destroy it way higher up in the sky."

"E-explosive magic?!" he yelled.

Tohka was right. Thanks to Yoshino, Kaguya, and Yuzuru, they'd managed to kill the speed of the satellite's descent, but it was still a bomb waiting to go off. If they let it detonate this close to the earth, the underground shelters wouldn't stand a chance.

"S-so then how do we—?" Shido muttered, pained.

"Keh-keh!" came Kaguya's voice from above. "It is of the utmost simplicity. If the machine cannot be destroyed below, then all that remains is to push it back into the heavens."

"Assent. That is the only way," Yuzuru said.

"Wha…? Can you do that?!" Shido asked, and the twins looked at each other briefly before grins popped up on their faces.

"Keh. Keh-keh… Have you forgotten our origins? We are the Yamais, children of the hurricane that cuts down all creation."

"Contract. Please let Yuzuru and Kaguya handle this. We will toss it like a scrap of paper."

They sounded more than confident, but Shido could see a faint sheen of sweat on their faces. It looked to him like they were putting on a show of bravado. Which made sense. Even with a lower-end estimate, the satellite must have weighed several tonnes. Plus, there was also the downward propulsion of the thrusters. It might have been a different story if they could have used their full power, but Shido had already sealed Kaguya's and Yuzuru's normal Spirit powers. They wouldn't have been able to carry the massive lump of metal up into the sky so easily as all that.

But without a word of complaint, the sisters nodded at each other before raising their hands at the same time.

"Hmph. Well then, shall we, Yuzuru?"

"Response. Ready when you are."

The wind swirling around the area increased in intensity to sweep up signs, street markers, and traffic lights, becoming a monstrous tornado.

"Ungh. Ahauuuuuuuuugh!"

"Vigor. Hi-yah!"

When the sisters threw their arms up, the satellite slowly—but surely—began to ascend.

"O-ohhh!" Shido felt himself clench his fists tighter. They might just be able to do it.

But then small missiles flew out of the sky toward the Yamai sisters and exploded behind them.

"Hyangh!"

"Anguish. Hngh!"

At the same time as the agonized cries of the Yamai sisters rang out above his head, the wind slackened, and the ascending satellite dropped down again onto the ice wall.

"Kaguya! Yuzuru!" Shido called out in a panic.

The lingering winds cleared away the puffs of smoke to reveal a pair of slightly charred twins. However limited their powers might have been, the fact that they had manifested their Astral Dress and had been shrouded in their winds had allowed them to survive the missile attack more or less unscathed.

"Ngh! Who is this villain that would dare obstruct us?!"

"Uncouth. This is unpleasant."

The Yamai sisters turned their glares toward the sky.

Shido followed their gazes upward and gasped. "Wha...?! Those are—!"

Off in the distant sky, countless Bandersnatches were flying toward Shido and the Spirits. He couldn't tell exactly how many there were, but from the look of the swarm, there had to be at least fifty of them. All with CR units attached to various limbs, all ready for war.

Which reminded him that there was a DEM airship up in the sky at the moment. Most likely, it had deployed this Bandersnatch squad to eliminate Shido and his friends and keep them from interfering with the satellite's crash to earth.

The Bandersnatches spread out in all directions. They attacked the Yamai sisters raising up the satellite, Yoshino preventing its descent, Miku amplifying everyone's strength with her song, and Tohka and Shido waiting to strike the decisive blow and destroy the would-be bomb.

"Ngh. Watch out!" Shido called to the Spirits, as the Bandersnatches launched micro missiles all at once.

But because they were all just barely holding the satellite up, the Spirits were hard-pressed to defend themselves against this barrage. Yoshino used her chilled air, the Yamais their wind, and Miku sound to create protective walls and try to deflect the attack, but more than one missile slipped past their defenses. Once one missile exploded, it ignited those around it, and the air shook as flames rolled out from the epicenter of the explosion.

"Eek!" Yoshino shrieked.

"Hngh!"

"Pain. Unnngh..."

The Yamai sisters groaned in unison.

"H-hey! What iiiiis this?!" Miku moaned.

The wall of ice and wind holding the satellite back creaked ominously.

"Everybody!" Shido shouted.

"Mm! You jerks!" Tohka, the only one who had knocked away every missile targeting her, narrowed her eyes sharply, crouched down, and then leaped into the air.

She raced forward to slice down the Bandersnatches attacking Yoshino and the others. "Now! Kaguya! Yuzuru! The satellite— Hngh!"

But there were too many enemies for her to take on alone. She was gradually pushed back by the Bandersnatches as they closed in on all sides, filling the gaps in their ranks with micro missiles and laser cannon blasts.

"Ungh!"

"Tohka! Hnrrr—," Shido shouted, and then leaped back. The reason was simple. One of the Bandersnatches was coming after him, brandishing a laser blade.

"Take this!" He tightened his grip of the hilt of his sword and swung Sandalphon. The Bandersnatch in front of him was neatly severed in two, and sparks sprayed out from the open cross section.

But the true terror of the Bandersnatches was their number and their coordination. With no regard for a fallen comrade and no fear of death, the dolls came charging in one after another.

"Ngh!" Shido dodged their attacks, deftly swung his blade, and kept counterattacking at any opening, but he soon reached his limit. His body cried out at the constant use of Sandalphon, and he fell to his knees.

Naturally, there was no way the Bandersnatches would show mercy or have compassion. The faceless death dealers closed in on Shido, not letting this favorable opportunity get away.

"Shido!" Tohka cried.

"Daaaarling?!" Miku wailed.

But the Spirits were also surrounded by too many Bandersnatches to count. They might have wanted to come to Shido's aid, but they were trapped themselves.

A Bandersnatch stood before Shido and raised its laser blade.

"Dammit!" he snarled.

"Shido!" As Tohka's voice rang out, the Bandersnatch brought its sword down toward Shido.

"Ike!"

In his suite at the Imperial Hotel East Tengu, Westcott heard his name out of nowhere and looked over his shoulder.

There was no door to the room behind him, however—only a massive window offering an exceptional view of the city of Tengu. Normally, he would not be hearing a voice calling to him from this direction.

But he soon realized what was going on when he turned around. Ellen had called to Westcott from the other side of a square hole in the impressive window-wall, hanging in the sky wearing a CR unit. Most likely, she hadn't wanted to waste time coming through the lobby and had flown directly to his room.

"If it isn't Ellen! Magnificent entrance, but perhaps your method of knocking could use a bit of refinement?" Westcott said, looking pointedly at the clean edges in the glass.

"We do not have time for jokes." Ellen came into the room through the hole in the window. "Please flee immediately. The rebel faction from the board meeting is planning to crash an artificial satellite onto your location."

"Ohhh, I heard. I got a call earlier as well." The corners of his lips turned up as he chuckled. "I honestly didn't think Murdock had it in him. Instead of sending an assassin, he uses a decommissioned satellite. Such a fun idea! Ah, perhaps I underestimated him. Wonderful resource. I will have to tell him exactly that when I get back to England."

"Ike," Ellen said flatly, displeased with his delight. "At any rate, you're in danger here. I will protect you with my Territory and fly as far as possible from this place. Please gather the things you will need."

Westcott shook his head. "We'll likely be fine right here. It's not going to amount to anything serious."

Ellen stared at him for a moment before speaking. "If you are with me, then it is indeed possible to minimize the damage with my Territory. However, I am speaking of the worst case."

"Oh, no, even before that, I expect that Murdock's plan will fail," Westcott said, and Ellen frowned dubiously.

"What do you mean?"

"Tengu is also home to one Shido Itsuka and the base for those Spirits who live on this side," he told her. "So firstly, I have no doubt whatsoever that Ratatoskr's airship is here. And that they will likely take care of this situation. We are talking about the organization Elliot created, after all."

"…" Ellen scowled the moment Elliot's name came up. "I find this incredible. Is that the reason you choose to stay here?"

"Mm. Is that wrong?" Westcott raised an eyebrow slightly.

"Obviously. Do you not understand your own importance?"

"Hmm…"

"Ike," Ellen said in a reproachful tone.

"All right." Westcott sighed before raising both hands in a gesture of defeat. "Then how about this? You're right, there is a worst case here. Murdock is meticulous. I wouldn't find it hard to believe that he has a backup and another backup for that one. So…" He turned away from Ellen back to the center of the room.

A girl was standing there silently.

"…let's dispatch her to the scene," he suggested.

Ellen frowned. "'Her'?"

"Yes. This is actually the perfect chance to take Mordred out for a test run," Westcott said. Then he asked the girl with a smile, "I'd like you to see what you're made of. How about it?"

"…"

The girl, of course, remained silent and merely nodded firmly.

"…"

Natsumi tried to get her ragged breathing under control.

Thump. Thump. Her heart had been pounding uncomfortably fast for a while now. The sound of it hit the insides of her ears like the footsteps of a giant.

The reason went without saying—Shido and his friends.

For a while there, it had been going great. It seemed that Tohka and the others had been evacuated, and after a call from Kotori, Shido headed obediently for a shelter. Everything was going exactly as Natsumi had hoped.

But then Shido suddenly started running back out into the city and began to try and stop the massive satellite. And now he had been driven into the tightest of all corners.

When he'd tried to push back the satellite with the friends who came to join him, a whole bunch of mechanical dolls called Bandersnatches appeared out of nowhere and began attacking them.

A Bandersnatch was pressing a blade down toward Shido, who was on his knees on the ground. In another second, that magic-imbued sword would fall and slice right through Shido's body. Natsumi remembered the agony when Ellen ripped into her stomach and shuddered unconsciously.

"Ah. Ah…"

And then Shido would definitely die. When she thought about that, Natsumi felt an even more intense pain in her heart.

"It's okay, you're okay," she murmured to herself reassuringly over and over. It would work out somehow. They didn't need someone like Natsumi to step up; there was no way Shido would die.

After all, everything had turned out fine when Shido was attacked in his home by Ellen. And Tohka and the others had come to save him when he was about to be crushed by the satellite. He had plenty of friends who would come to his rescue. There was no place for Natsumi here, not now.

"It's okay… I mean, someone'll save him, right? Hurry up already," Natsumi said in a small voice, as she waited for someone to rescue Shido.

But Tohka, Yoshino, the Yamai sisters, and Miku all had their hands full dealing with the Bandersnatches. On top of that, she felt like someone had said something about Kotori and her crew being in a battle in the sky.

"Hurry... Someone... Come on." Natsumi screwed up her face at the pain of her pounding heart, but nobody showed up.

The Bandersnatch brought its sword down on Shido.

"Someone... Someone!"

In that instant, Natsumi finally realized that there was only one someone there.

"Wha...?!" Shido's eyes flew open in surprise.

Right as the Bandersnatch's sword came hurtling at him and he started to give up hope, helpless as he was, something squirmed in his pocket.

For a second, he thought it was his phone. But it wasn't. The Chupa Chups he'd picked up in the underground facility leaped from his pocket and protected him from the Bandersnatch blade with its small body.

"Huh...? A-a lollipop?" He gaped.

And of course he did. A sphere small enough to fit in his palm was floating before him and holding back the blow of a laser blade, sending crackling magical energy in every direction. This was the sort of thing that caught people by surprise.

The Chupa Chups repelled the sword and smashed in the head of the Bandersnatch before beginning to glow. And then the tiny silhouette gradually grew bigger.

A few seconds later, it turned into a small girl clad in an Astral Dress like a witch's costume.

"N-Natsumi?!" Shido cried.

Yes. This was the Spirit he had been running around town looking for.

He'd guessed that if she was still above ground, she'd be somewhere she could keep an eye on him, but he never imagined that she'd been hiding so close by.

"Natsumi, you…," he said.

Natsumi parted her lips, without meeting his eyes. "…and do it."

"Huh?"

"Hurry up and do it," she said, hiding her face with the brim of her hat, as she turned her back to him. "You're smashing that big thing, right?"

This was all Shido needed to hear. Of course, there was the fact that he had another powerful ally in a tight spot. But more than that, he was practically over the moon that the very same Natsumi who'd steadfastly refused to open up to him and his friends had, for whatever reason, voluntarily come to him and said she would help.

"You got that right!" Shido nodded vigorously and tightened his grip on Sandalphon.

However.

"Eeeaaah!"

He had no sooner heard Miku scream behind him than the brave March she had been playing was abruptly cut off. The Bandersnatch attack had separated her from her keyboard now. She leaped backward and began attacking the herd of Bandersnatches with her voice.

At the same time as the bolstering music faded away, cracks appeared in the wall of ice that was just barely holding back the satellite, and pieces of the wall began to crumble as the swirling winds lost their force.

"Wha…?!"

Yoshino and the Yamai sisters had been bolstered by Miku's performance, and without it, they weren't able to maintain the wall while fighting the Bandersnatches at the same time.

No longer obstructed, the satellite began to accelerate once more and plummet toward the ground.

"Shido!" After slashing away the Bandersnatches in the air, Tohka descended to stand by Shido and Natsumi. She looked at Natsumi in surprise before turning her eyes on Shido with a gasp. "You okay, Shido?!"

"Y-yeah... I'm okay. What's more important..."

When she saw him peering up at the falling satellite, Tohka nodded, a hint of fear on her face.

"I know. But what are we supposed to do?!" she said, panicked. "If we destroy it here, there'll be a huge explosion, right?!"

"Hmph." Natsumi sniffed. "It's fine. Go ahead and crush it. I mean, you've got these amazing swords and all, don't you?"

"No, it's got this explosive magic—," Shido started, and Natsumi snorted again grumpily.

"Hmph." She thrust her right hand out and shouted, "Haniel!"

The broom-shaped Angel appeared in her hand, the sweeping end opened up, and a dazzling light enveloped the area.

"Whoa?!"

"Mm?!"

Shido and Tohka instinctively shielded their eyes.

And then when they could see again...

"Wha—?" Shido looked up at the sky, and his eyes grew round as saucers at the contrast from just a moment earlier.

But that was only natural. Whatever else, the satellite that had been closing in on the ground several hundred meters below was now an enormous, chubby pig mascot.

This had to have been due to Haniel's transformation power. Shido gasped and looked at Natsumi.

He recalled the first time he met Natsumi in mid-October. Just like now, she had changed the charging AST members into mascots and the whistling missiles into carrots. And even when those carrot missiles hit the ground, the explosions were nothing more than the funny kind found in manga.

Of course, given the serious difference in power and size, this wasn't exactly the same, but maybe now...!

"C'mon. Hurry and do it already!" Natsumi said with annoyance.

The enormous pig was still hurtling toward the city of Tengu. Its power as an explosive might have been extremely reduced, but the size of it alone would still produce a tremendous impact if it hit the ground.

But that didn't change the fact that they could now destroy the target right here. Shido said a brief thank-you to Natsumi and looked over at Tohka.

"Let's go, Tohka!"

"Mm! Ready when you are!"

Shido and Tohka nodded at each other, then brandished identical Sandalphons at the target simultaneously.

An Angel that there was normally only one of. A "miracle made manifest" that should never have faced itself.

Shido and Tohka swung those miracles as one.

"Yaaaaaaaaah!"

"Haaaaaaaaah!"

Their glittering slicing attacks crossed in the air and ripped into the target.

But even in its new shape, the giant pig apparently still possessed its abilities as a Bandersnatch; it tried to stretch out a Territory and defend against this dual attack.

"Ngh!"

This was the blow of an Angel. The pig wouldn't be able to guard against it so easily with just a Bandersnatch's Territory. But Tohka had also been worn down in the fight with the death-dealing dolls. And due to repeated hard use, rather than the Angel itself, the person handling it—Shido—had reached his limits.

At the last second, their attacks were unable to break through the Territory and merely closed around the pig as if pushing it forward.

"Hngh!"

A little more. Their attack just needed one last push. But they could not fill in that last little bit, no matter how they tried.

Yoshino, Kaguya, Yuzuru, Miku. If he and Tohka had help from even just one of them, they probably could have broken through. But those Spirits were still blocked off by the Bandersnatches and unable to make a move.

"Like this…we—" Shido was about to drop to his knees, a look of anguish on his face.

"Haniel!" Natsumi brandished the Angel in her right hand and cried out once more.

After seeing that Shido and Tohka couldn't smash the pig, was Natsumi actually going to change it into something else? No. If that were possible, she would've done that to start with. So then what exactly…?

While Shido was wondering this, Natsumi continued to cry out. "Kaleidoscope!"

Instantly, a strange color bled across the broom-shaped Angel, giving it a sheen like the surface of a polished mirror, and the broom itself was transformed into what appeared to be a lump of clay.

And then a heartbeat later.

"Huh?!" Shido's eyes widened at what he saw in Natsumi's hand.

It was a sword. A wide blade about as tall as Natsumi. With a shining golden cross guard and a jet-black grip.

Yes. She had manifested the Angel Sandalphon.

"What are you doing to Shido?! The only one who gets to play tricks on him…is meeeeeeeeee!" she shouted, and swung Sandalphon at the pig with all her might.

"Sandalphon!"

Light jetted from the blade and flew toward the target in a slicing attack as if following along the arc of Natsumi's sword.

The sword didn't just look like Tohka's Angel. Although it wasn't as strong as Tohka's, this was undoubtedly the same type of power as the real Sandalphon.

Shido, Tohka, and now Natsumi.

Attacks from three Sandalphons rained down on the target's Territory. The invisible wall around the pig made a cracking sound and then shattered to pieces.

With its Territory destroyed, there was nothing left to protect the enormous pig. The aftershocks of the triple attack knocked the pig back with a funny sound effect like something out of a manga, and then countless Chupa Chups began to fall like rain.

"Shido…!"

"Keh-keh! You have accomplished it!"

"Assent. That was amazing."

"Aaah, daaaarling, you're so brilliant!"

After Shido, Tohka, and Natsumi succeeded in destroying the satellite, Yoshino, Kaguya, Yuzuru, and Miku ran over to them, having at last defeated the army of Bandersnatches. Although they all had cuts and scratches, fortunately none of the girls were seriously injured.

Shido let out a sigh of relief before bowing deeply. "All of you… Thanks. If it had been just me…I wouldn't have been able to save the people in the city. Seriously, thank you."

The girls all shook their heads.

"I told you, Shido," Tohka said simply. "You saved all of us first."

"We. Love…this city. Too."

"Heh-heh-heh! Dang straight. You gotta let us help this much at least."

"Heh. Well, without your presence from the very outset, we would not be here in this moment."

"Conformity. We still owe you a debt."

"That's riiiight. In fact, you turning to me for help, daaarling, it makes me so happy that I feel like I could write a new song."

The girls grinned at him, and Shido returned a pained smile. He said thank you again.

But in the midst of this, one person alone was trying to sneak away without saying a word—Natsumi.

"Natsumi!" Shido called out to her.

"…!" Natsumi jumped noticeably and came to a stop. And then she hesitantly turned back to Shido and the others and sniffed in a somewhat timid manner. "Wh-what? You gonna tell me that I should've come out before the eleventh hour? Or that it was creepy for me to turn into a lollipop and hide in your pocket this whole time?"

Shido smiled slightly at this now-familiar negative song and dance and let out a short sigh of relief. "I'm glad you're okay."

"Huh...?" Her eyes grew wide, and she froze in place. "Wh-what... are you talking about? I...went and hid... And you worked so hard..."

Natsumi stammered as her body began to tremble.

"And...I—I did such terrible things to all of you... So why... Why...?"

Sobs steadily made their way into her voice. Fat tears spilled from her emerald eyes, and she continued, practically shouting.

"What... What is *with* you...? All of you! Are you stupid, a bunch of idiots?! I don't get it...! Why would you...?!"

The last part was no longer words. Tears streamed down her face, and she began to wail.

"Ungh... Aah... *Hic!* Aah... Waaaaaaaaah!"

"Wh-whoa, Natsumi." Shido had not expected her to cry on him. Unsure what to do, he waved his hands back and forth to try and placate her.

Tohka and the other Spirits also stepped forward to try and soothe Natsumi.

But her tears did not stop.

"I-I'm! Sorry!" she cried. "I did all that bad stuff...made trouble for everybody... I'm sorry! And you were all so nice to me... But I only ever said mean things—I'm sorry...!"

Hiccuping the whole while, Natsumi talked. She kept going, as if the many emotions that had been building up inside her were spilling out all at once.

"I was so happy when...you gave me a massage... Happy you...cut my hair...and picked out clothes... I was happy...you made me up... I was so happy...you said I looked cute!"

She sniffled.

"I was so happy...but I couldn't tell you then... I'm sorry...!"

Natsumi looked at Shido with puffy, red eyes.

"Thank...you..."

Shido's own eyes widened in surprise, while Tohka and the other Spirits looked at one another with identical expressions of surprise.

But his face quickly softened into a smile as he turned to Natsumi.

"Don't worry about it. I should be thanking you. If you hadn't been here, I don't know what would've happened to us."

"You don't have to worry about that, either." Natsumi sniffed. "You did that stuff for me first and all."

"Yeah?" Shido said, exhaled at last, and held out his hand.

"Huh?" Natsumi stared in surprise.

Shido felt embarrassed somehow at her reaction. He scratched his head awkwardly and opened his mouth again. "Umm. It's, uh, you know. I promised that when this was all over, you could go wherever you wanted. And I can't stop you anyway, but if you'd like…" Now he looked Natsumi in the eyes. "Maybe you could…be my friend?"

"…!" Natsumi gasped, stunned, and looked at Shido and the girls behind him in turn. And then very slowly, timidly, she took his hand and nodded.

"Ungh… Ungh… Ungh… Waaaaaah! Waaaaaaaah!" She started to cry once more, rivers of tears pouring down her cheeks.

"Aaah! Daaarling! You went and made Natsumi cry again!" Miku said, grinning maliciously.

"H-huh?!" Shido jumped.

"I simply can't truuuust Natsumi to a person like you, hmm? So, Natsumi, let's you and me be friends, too!"

"Mm! Shido, you can't pick on Natsumi," Tohka admonished him. "I'll be her friend, too!"

"Uh. Um… So… M-me too…" Yoshino looked at the Witch Spirit shyly.

"Yoshinon's in! Yoshinon wants a piece of the friendship pie!"

"Keh-keh! So the danger lies in leaving the self to Shido?" Kaguya said. "Very well, Natsumi. As a special patronage, I shall make you my retainer."

"Assent." Yuzuru nodded. "We don't know what kind of perverted games Shido will force upon you. We should protect you carefully."

The other Spirits also started to crowd around Natsumi, and Shido cried out helplessly.

"H-hey, you guys! Don't go giving her the wrong idea about me!"

The girls all burst out laughing.

When he glanced over at Natsumi, he saw a new look on her face, tearstained though it was.

She was smiling very adorably.

Epilogue
Friend or Enemy

About thirty minutes after the satellite had been safely shot down, Shido got a message from Kotori, who had been engaged in battle in the sky above Tengu with a DEM airship. Apparently, while the enemy ship had given them the slip, *Fraxinus* had made it out with relatively little damage.

But the transporter was apparently temporarily out of order, and so Shido and the Spirits were walking over to the underground facility before the evacuated citizens came out from their shelters.

Shido's body, damaged by the use of the Angel, had recovered enough after a brief rest that he could at least manage to walk. Even so, a worried Tohka had pestered him to let her carry him on her back. Though there was no one around, this was still embarrassing, so he had politely declined.

In the end, Natsumi decided to come with Shido and the others to Ratatoskr. Of course, her Spirit powers were still not sealed, and he hadn't explained that whole situation to her yet. He could easily imagine that Natsumi would not want to lose the powers of transformation she used like second nature.

Nonetheless, he was sure if he took the time to persuade her, she would come around. He glanced over at her walking next to him.

"..."

"Wh-what?" she asked, baffled. But he caught no glimpse of the harshness that had been on her face previously.

He shook his head, a smile crossing his lips. "No, it's nothing."

"Oh. Fine," she said curtly, and twisted her head away.

But before too long, Natsumi started speaking to Shido this time, in a whisper so that Tohka and the others up ahead couldn't hear her. "So, like."

"Hmm?" He raised an eyebrow. "What's up, Natsumi?"

"It's just…I wanted to ask you something. That okay?"

"Sure. What is it?" he replied, and she tugged on his sleeve silently. "Ah! Hey! What're you doing all of a sudden?"

"It's fine. Just come." She dragged him into a nearby alley. And then staring hard at him, she asked with a strange look on her face, "Hey, Shido?"

"Wh-what?" Her unusual behavior was making him nervous.

"I…" Natsumi swallowed hard before continuing. "Am I really cute?"

"Huh?" Shido's eyes grew wider at the unexpected question.

But when he really thought about it, it was basically the same as the question she'd posed him the first time they met. Well, naturally, the Natsumi then had been in the form of an adult woman, though.

His face relaxing into a smile, Shido nodded firmly. "Yeah, of course. You're very cute, Natsumi."

"…!" She reddened and opened her eyes as she continued in a halting fashion. "Later…"

"Later?"

"Um… Will you…teach me…makeup?" she asked, hanging her head in embarrassment.

"Sure, you bet." Shido nodded firmly once more. "I'm sure you'll get the hang of it right away."

"…Yeah?" Natsumi nodded, as if she was finally convinced.

And then.

"Huh?" Shido let out a bewildered cry.

But that was only natural. Because Natsumi had abruptly reached out to yank on Shido's collar and pull his face down.

Lips met lips.

"…?!"

Indeed, he knew he would have to explain the situation to Natsumi and kiss her in order to lock away her Spirit powers. But this was so out of the blue, he wasn't mentally prepared. His eyes flitted about in confusion.

In the next moment, Shido felt something warm flowing into his body, and at the same time, the witchy Astral Dress Natsumi was wearing melted into particles of light and faded away.

"Ah?! Wh-what's going on…?" Shock colored her face, and she crouched down on the spot, covering her chest with her arms. Her face beet red, she muttered, "I—I had no idea. So when you seal my Spirit power, my Astral Dress disappears."

Waving his hands in a panic, Shido hurriedly said, "Y-yeah, the Astral Dress is made of Spirit power, I guess, so— Wait. Natsumi? How do you know about the whole sealing—?"

"Aah!" Tohka yelped from behind.

Apparently, she had come back because Shido and Natsumi had disappeared. Naturally, it wasn't only Tohka; Yoshino, the Yamai sisters, and Miku were also standing there.

"Shido! What are you doing?!"

"…! Uh. Um… I'm not. Looking…"

"Keh-keh! I must commend your perversion to seal her in the middle of town in this way."

"Assent. Your desire must be quite incredible to make use of the abnormal space of the deserted city for your little games."

"Eek! Daaarling, you're so booold!"

And so they began to make a fuss in this fashion.

"H-hang on a sec! I didn't start this—" Shido tried to plead his case, but the Spirits weren't having it.

"It failed?!" Murdock half shrieked at the news that arrived at the conference room of DEM Industries' UK head office.

The faces of the board of directors assembled there paled.

But that was to be expected. They had participated in a failed assassination attempt on Isaac Westcott. In other words, this meant that the hatred and murderous desire they felt toward him would be returned to them as is—no, multiplied several times over.

"Wh-what is the meaning of this, Murdock?! We went along with this plan because you said it was a sure thing!"

"Exactly! How do you intend to fix this?!"

"I-I'm not a part of this! It was all Murdock, out of control!"

The middle-aged men cried out pathetically, slamming their fists against the table. It was quite the amusing sight, but Murdock was in no mood for laughing.

He was indeed the ringleader in this attempt at assassination. This was an indisputable fact. And if it reached Westcott's ears, then Murdock—no, the whole of his faction would be facing Westcott's ire.

"..."

But everything wasn't necessarily over. Murdock pulled the mic on the table toward him and spoke to the bridge of the large airship *Heptameron*, which had been dispatched to Tengu.

"Not yet," he said. "It's not been decided yet, Captain. Is *Heptameron* all right?!"

"*Yes, sir! We did engage in combat with the Ratatoskr ship, but less than ten percent of the hull was damaged.*"

"In that case, we still have one final *Humpty-Dumpty*, yes?!"

The eyebrows of the directors in the room all jumped up at Murdock's words.

Yes. The deeply cautious Murdock had readied for this mission three *Humpty-Dumpty* units. The first was *First Egg*, bait to lure in the Ratatoskr airship. The second was the actual main component of the plan to end the life of Westcott, *Second Egg*. And there was one more.

The third *Humpty-Dumpty* had been made available in case the mission ended in a misfire. The final machine—*Third Egg*—was equipped on *Heptameron*. Naturally, it wasn't the case that a full satellite was attached to the airship or that the ship could drop it from geostationary orbit. Compared with *First* and *Second*, *Third* boasted far less power.

But even so, if they could detonate it directly above Westcott, its explosive magic alone would be enough to blow away Westcott and the shelter along with him.

"What is MD Westcott's current location?!" Murdock demanded.

"Currently...it appears that he's still in his hotel room."

"What?!" Murdock twisted his face up in disbelief. Westcott hadn't fled to an underground shelter with all this going on?

He was overcome with an inexpressible frustration. He felt like this man was sneering at the plan that Murdock had poured his heart and soul into.

But that didn't change the fact that this was an excellent opportunity. If he hadn't fled to a shelter, then it was possible that the power of *Third Egg* was more than enough to take him down.

"Well, then." Murdock issued his instructions into the mic. "I don't care how much of the city is destroyed. Take Westcott's head."

"...?!"

Having given Natsumi his jacket when she found herself half naked because of the sealing of her powers, and now back on the road to the underground facility, Shido abruptly pressed his ear and frowned.

The reason was simple. A shrill alarm was ringing through the earpiece he was wearing.

"Wh-what's going on, Kotori?" he asked, and he soon heard her panicked voice.

"We've detected a magic signal in the sky! It's an explosive-magic signal from the airship that got away from us before!"

"What?!" He gasped and turned his eyes toward the sky.

"Mm? What's wrong, Shido?"

Perhaps suspicious of this change in Shido, Tohka and the others cocked their heads to one side.

Without taking his eyes off the sky, Shido opened his mouth. "Yeah. I guess it's not actually over, after all. Another bomb like the ones before is going to drop."

"Wha...?!"

They all grew tense. And then like Shido, they turned their eyes to the sky as if ready to once again shoot down the embodiment of murderous intent that was about to fall from above.

But he had only just sealed Natsumi's Spirit powers and her key ability of transformation, and the rest of the Spirits were completely worn out. It would be difficult, to say the least, to intercept another falling target in their current condition.

However, they had no choice but to do it. Shido calmed himself down again the way he had before and concentrated on his right hand.

But before Sandalphon could manifest, an intense pain raced through his entire body and brought him to his knees.

"Ngah!"

"Shido!" Tohka ran over to him, worried.

But the enemy wouldn't care a bit about Shido's condition. He heard another alarm over his earpiece.

"Commander! A Bandersnatch equipped with explosive magic has been released from the airship!"

"Can Fraxinus *counterattack?!"*

"It's impossible from this position!"

"Ngh! Turn about immediately! We have to do something before it hits—"

In the middle of Kotori's order, Shido saw a beam of light in the sky, and then there was a massive explosion above the city of Tengu. The air around them crackled.

"Wha?!" Shido and the Spirits gaped, and he heard the voices of the crew through his earpiece.

"The signal's...vanished!"

"What? Did it self-destruct?"

"I—I don't know. But immediately before the explosion, a heat source—"

A heat source. Shido recalled the beam of light he'd just seen. Someone couldn't have actually shot down the explosive?

That line of thought did make sense. But someone who could destroy with a single shot the same kind of device that Shido and his friends had been forced to combine forces to destroy...

"...!"

He shifted his gaze to the left, the direction the beam had come from. He could see a human figure there.

"That's..."

The shadow slowly approached Shido and the others and then stopped in midair.

It was a Wizard wearing a CR unit. And not an AST unit. A wiring suit with a design that closely resembled the one Ellen wore, equipped with distinctive thrusters and a massive magic gun.

"Wha—?" Shido's jaw dropped when he saw her.

He was certainly surprised at a DEM Wizard attacking a DEM bomb. And at the fact that she had the power to annihilate in one blow what it had taken the combined might of several Spirits—albeit in a sealed state—to destroy.

But what stole the larger part of Shido's attention was a much simpler phenomenon.

He knew this Wizard.

"Ori...gami...?" he said tentatively.

The Wizard—Origami—looked silently at Shido and the Spirits, with eyes just like always— No. With eyes even more unreadable than usual.

Afterword

It's been a while! This is Koushi Tachibana. I'm bringing you *Date A Live, Vol. 9: Change Natsumi*. How did you like it? I do hope you enjoyed the book.

Naturally, the cover features Natsumi (the real one). The young-woman version of Volume 8 was marvelous, but the real Natsumi we meet this volume is also a delight. I think the messy hair and the disgruntled expression are a most powerful combination. (This is my personal feeling, and there may be differences in how this is taken.) I really love characters whose personalities lean negative, so I had a lot of fun writing this.

In terms of design, it's so interesting how the emeralds on the hat of Natsumi (real) seem like raw, unpolished gems in contrast with the emerald on the hat of Natsumi (grown-up). And the Kotori from the color pages—I never even imagined her jacket could be used in this way. Tsunako is honestly amazing for incorporating these chic little details into these images I'm communicating.

And so here we are with Volume 9. This is unknown territory for me, given that my debut series was complete in eight volumes. And *Date A Live* is expected to continue further, so look forward to Volume 10. Two digits is a serious milestone. My light novel license is for automatics only, so I shouldn't be able to write anything beyond Volume 9. I will be okay, though, right? I'm pretty sure I heard that you have to offer up sweet treats to the god of light novels (a blond pig-tailed tsundere) when proceeding to Volume 10 and beyond in a series without a license. If you write more than ten volumes without doing so, the god of light novels (a blond pigtailed tsundere) comes at you night after night, cheeks puffed up in a pout, saying, "The nerve, to write ten volumes without my permission!" as she jabs you in the gut. Aah, I really am going to write ten volumes without a license.

Now then, about the manga version of *Date A Live* I told you about before, the serialization finally began in *Monthly Shonen Ace* (on sale November 26)! It's coming to you with a cover page, color illustrations, and extra pages for the first chapter! Please do check out this new *Date A Live* drawn by Sekihiko Inui!

And the second season of the anime is also proceeding apace, so enjoy! The design of this and that are amazing. Eh-heh-heh!

Once again, this book was produced thanks to Tsunako, my editor, and everyone involved in the publication and distribution of this book. Thank you so much.

The next volume—*Date A Live*, Vol. 10—will have that character decorating the cover at last. I'm expecting some big moves in the story, so I hope you will all look forward to that.

Well then, I hope that we will meet again in the next volume.

Koushi Tachibana
October 2013

HAVE YOU BEEN TURNED ON TO LIGHT NOVELS YET?

86—EIGHTY-SIX, VOL. 1-11

In truth, there is no such thing as a bloodless war. Beyond the fortified walls protecting the eighty-five Republic Sectors lies the "nonexistent" Eighty-Sixth Sector. The young men and women of this forsaken land are branded the Eighty-Six and, stripped of their humanity, pilot "unmanned" weapons into battle...

Manga adaptation available now!

WOLF & PARCHMENT, VOL. 1-6

The young man Col dreams of one day joining the holy clergy and departs on a journey from the bathhouse, Spice and Wolf. Winfiel Kingdom's prince has invited him to help correct the sins of the Church. But as his travels begin, Col discovers in his luggage a young girl with a wolf's ears and tail named Myuri, who stowed away for the ride!

Manga adaptation available now!

SOLO LEVELING, VOL. 1-7

E-rank hunter Jinwoo Sung has no money, no talent, and no prospects to speak of—and apparently, no luck, either! When he enters a hidden double dungeon one fateful day, he's abandoned by his party and left to die at the hands of some of the most horrific monsters he's ever encountered.

Comic adaptation available now!